Along Came A Spider

Rod Randall

Created by Paul Buchanan and Rod Randall

Nashville, Tennessee

0–8054–1981–0

Published by Broadman & Holman Publishers, Nashville, Tennessee
Editorial Team: Vicki Crumpton, Janis Whipple, Kim Overcash
Typesetting: SL Editorial Services

Dewey Decimal Classification: Fiction
Subject Heading: BROTHERS AND SISTERS—FICTION / TREE HOUSES—FICTION / CHRISTIAN LIFE—FICTION
Library of Congress Card Catalog Number: 99–042992

Library of Congress Cataloging-in-Publication Data

Randall, Rod, 1962–
Along came a spider / Rod Randall.
p. cm.—(HeebieJeebies series ; v. 7)
Summary: When Jaime and her brother discover an abandoned tree house overrun with spiders, they embark on an all-out war against nature before finally learning to accept all of God's creatures.
ISBN 0–8054–1981–0 (pb)
[1. Spiders—Fiction. 2. Tree houses—Fiction. 3. Brothers and sisters—Fiction. 4. Christian life—Fiction. 5. Horror stories.]
I. Title. II. HeebieJeebies series ; v. 7.
PZ7.R15825 Al 2000
[Fic]—dc21

99–042992
CIP

1 2 3 4 5 04 03 02 01 00

DEDICATION

For the best of friends,
Tom and Marcia Stewart,
Grant, Wilson, Jackson, and Grace

Chapter 1

I've been scared before, but nothing like when we moved. A magnolia tree loomed over our new neighborhood like a dark green cloud, twice the height of the oaks and elms around it. They were tall by normal standards, but the magnolia tree dwarfed them.

I followed my older brother to the roots of the massive trunk. Twenty feet up, the huge branches split in three directions around a weathered tree house. Other platforms and rooms rested on limbs at different points.

"Check out the mag tree," Conner marvelled. "It's like a tree town up there." He wove his fingers together and cracked his knuckles. "We've *got* to climb this one, Sis."

"Now?" I checked my watch. The short hand angled past seven.

Conner scanned the tree from bottom to top. His chin dropped. "Come on, Jaime. What else are we going to do?"

"Go home. Unpack." I had clothes to put away. A closet to organize. So did Conner.

He stepped on a wood rung nailed to the trunk and grabbed another above his head. "Are you coming or not?" Before I could answer, he lifted himself from the ground. The wood boards wrapped around the trunk like a spiral staircase.

"The steps are rotten, Conner," I called up to him. "And it's getting dark."

He ignored me.

I circled the tree, watching my brother. "I'll tell Mom and Dad where I last saw you. And how I tried to warn—"

"Go ahead," he interrupted.

"And how I never saw you again." I paused for my brother's next wisecrack. Conner spoke with his shoes, stepping from one rung to the next. With my neck doubled back, I felt like I was standing beneath the world's largest natural canopy. Limbs, branches, and twigs grew in every direction. The leaves were hand-sized and shiny, like plastic. They numbered in the millions and hid the sky. I wondered if, even on its best day, the sun could penetrate the one-tree forest above me.

"This is awesome!" Conner blurted out. He disappeared into the tree house. Seconds later, his blond head poked through the window. "Come on, Jaime. Check it out."

I crossed my arms. I could see the top story of our house from where I stood. Just thinking about what I *wasn't* getting done made me feel guilty.

"Chicken-n-n-n . . . Chicken-n-n-n," Conner chanted.

I debated. I had nothing against climbing. Or tree houses. Normally, I would have been right behind him. But when I left my old, familiar home, I left my confidence with it. I had too many adjustments to make. A new town (totally creepy). A new house (really ancient). And new friends (if I could make some).

Conner went poultry on me. "Bawk. Bawk-bawk."

"Bawk yourself," I yelled back. I grabbed a board and pulled myself up. In a month, I'd begin high school—with or without friends. Time to get tough. I wasn't the bravest kid on earth, but I wasn't a chicken either. Conner was only two years older than me. If he could climb it, so could I.

"Hurry up," my brother called down.

I picked up the pace. Rusty nails held the slats in place, and the wood felt like it would crumble in my hands. But I kept going. Five feet. Ten. My hair fell in my eyes. I paused to brush it aside, then continued. But I didn't get far.

A speckled brown spider scurried over my hand.

"Gross!" I shrieked, flinging it into the air.

"That's a quarter," Conner shouted. A while ago, my parents got sick and tired of me using the word "gross." They imposed a twenty-five-cent fine for every time I said it. When they caught me, I usually responded by saying "gross" again, which immediately put me deeper in the hole.

"No way. It was a spider. A *spider!*"

"Not a *spider?!*" Conner mocked. "How *gross!*"

"But it was!"

"Sorry, Miss Muffet. You owe."

"Sorry, Miss Muffet, you owe," I mimicked, using my baby voice. My parents overdid it with the "fine" thing. But they definitely had a point. I got my mileage out of "gross." Sometimes I said it with two syllables, as in *ga-ross*. Other times I hissed my esses like a snake. But so did my friends, and they didn't get fined a quarter.

I examined the rungs and trunk before starting again. The tree house was only a few more feet above me. Pretty soon, I climbed through the floor hatch and stood up inside. The main tree house compared in size to a small bedroom, but with a lower ceiling. A scrap of carpet covered the floor. The walls were gray plywood. No paint. No posters. I did a slow three-sixty, taking note of what owned the corners. Cobwebs.

"Come out here," Conner said.

He didn't have to ask twice. I edged through a door that led to a view deck. A railing secured half of it. The rest was open like a diving platform.

"We'll make this railing our first project," Conner said. He admired the rooms and decks throughout the giant tree. "I can't believe someone would give up on this place."

I couldn't either. It was a tree city all right. Ropes, planks, and ladders connected the rooms, which came in all shapes and sizes. Some had roofs, some had walls, some rails. Some were nothing more than platforms nailed to branches.

"Let's check it out," Conner said. He climbed like an ape up one of the limbs. I watched him for a minute, then went back inside. A fuzzy, gray spider scurried for a crack in the wood. It got there before I could flatten it. I studied the dark crevice, wondering how many other spiders were in there. That's when I noticed that half of the wall had been varnished. Only half.

Weird. Another unfinished detail.

When I returned to the deck, Conner was out of sight. "Conner?"

No answer. I moved with caution along the limb he had taken. My fingernails snagged on the rough bark. I edged higher. Suddenly, a branch moved beneath my hand. I watched in horror as an eight-legged leaf crawled from the spot I was holding. "Gross!" I screamed. I knew from science class that eight legs could only mean one thing. It wasn't a lizard. Or a moth. Or an insect. It was a spider.

I yelled for Conner to help. He didn't answer. He didn't even say anything about me owing another quarter.

"Conner?" I called out. "Are you all right?"

I heard a slap through the dense foliage. Skin against skin.

I searched the dark, upper branches. "Conner, what happened? What's wrong?"

I heard movement far above me. Leaves shaking together. Denim sliding on bark.

"Never mind," Conner finally said.

I wouldn't let up. "It was a spider, wasn't it?"

"It's dead now. Who cares?"

"Did it bite you?"

Conner slid down a rope to the platform I was sitting on. The loose rail made me nervous. One wrong step and I'd be toast. A smear of spider legs and guts painted Conner's neck. So did blood.

"Gro—," I caught myself in time. I stretched his shirt collar to get a better look. "It did bite you, huh?"

"Maybe."

"It's already swollen."

Conner softly touched his neck. "Not much."

"Not yet," I countered. "Let's get out of here."

Conner scanned the far reaches of the tree, lingering over the half-finished rooms and decks. I could tell he didn't want to leave. "Stupid spider."

"Come on," I told him. I started down. "Stay above me. If you pass out, I'll catch you."

"Pass out? Sure." Conner laid on the tough-guy attitude. But when he touched his neck, he winced.

We carefully worked our way down, avoiding spiders and webs all the way. It seemed the number of them had doubled since we first climbed the tree. I figured we were home free when we reached the main tree house. I soon found out otherwise. When I poked my head in through the doorway, I saw a web stretched from one wall to the next in the pattern of a wheel. The silk strands looked as strong as spokes. The spider in the hub had a seven-inch leg span. Bands of orange and black alternated along its spiny legs. I kept my mouth shut and eased back to the porch.

"What's wrong?" Conner grumbled, still in his tough-guy mode.

"You don't want to know." I looked for a way down other than through the main house. There wasn't one. The hatch in the floor was the only route to the ladder that spiraled down the trunk. I stepped back inside. The giant spider had a cone-shaped body. Legs like a skeleton's fingers. Deadly fangs. It fixed eight eyes on me and raised its front legs, as if to say, "One wrong move and you're mine."

Chapter 2

My brother shoved me aside and went for the spider. "Just knock it down." He raised a shoe and kicked at the web. It came loose just as a breeze swirled through the main house. The web with the giant spider floated like a sail into my hair.

"GROSS!" I screamed. "GET IT OFF!" I twisted and clawed at the white silk. It felt like sticky nylon. The spider crawled along my arm, then jumped to my face. "AHHH!"

Conner slapped me twice but missed. I flung the spider from my face and rushed to the outer deck with the web still stuck in my hair.

"Where is it?" I asked, freaking out.

Conner remained in the house. He poked his head through one of the windows. "It went out there. I lost it."

"You're sure it's not on me?" I did a three-sixty. I folded my arms in close and buried my fists in my chin.

"Positive," Conner said. He watched me squirm. "By the way. I heard you earlier. That's four violations. You owe a buck."

I went inside the main house, grumbling. I lowered myself through the hole in the floor. Conner followed. We were halfway down when I heard a branch bend near the top of the tree. Leaves rustled. "What was that?"

Conner didn't answer me. He kept touching his neck and closing his eyes.

I continued down, keeping one eye on Conner and the other on the upper branches. I couldn't imagine a spider heavy enough to shake a branch. But everything about the tree was giant.

Solid ground never felt so good. Conner and I took a last look at the tree house, then headed home. As we walked away, more sounds came from the tree. Branches dipped. Something scraped the bark. The sounds followed us, from one tree to the next. I kept turning around, but never in time. Conner watched his steps, dazed.

"No wonder they quit building," I muttered. "That tree's haunted."

"I'm coming back," Conner said.

"What? You saw all those spiders. What if they're poisonous? The venom from a black widow can kill you."

Conner laughed at me. "Thanks for the warning, Miss Muffet."

"Knock it off."

"Next time, I'll wear gloves and bring a hammer and kill every spider in that tree. There. Problem solved. After that, I'll finish the tree house—with or without you."

I stared at my brother's neck, fearing what the venom might do. "You're not serious?"

He was.

My mom had a fit at the sight of Conner's bite. "We're going to emergency."

Conner rolled his eyes. "Emergency?"

My mom went for her purse and keys.

"I'm fine," Conner told her. He was Mr. Confident, especially around the family.

Mom took another look at his neck, then pushed open the front door. "Better safe than sorry."

I offered to tag along, but my mom wanted me to wait for my dad to get home from work and tell him what happened. So I did. Alone.

I went to my room to put stuff away. I emptied a box of books and arranged them by author on the shelf. I hung dresses in the closet. But all the while I kept remembering the tree and the spiders. I pictured their legs. Long. Spiny. I pictured their bodies. Black. Brown. Striped. Hairy. I pictured their fangs. Deadly.

Being alone in our house didn't help. My dad wouldn't admit it, but I think he bought it from the Addams family. Our house was older than everyone in the family combined. And big. It was a three-story Victorian that dated back to the 1850s. According to my dad, it had the kind of attention to detail you don't see anymore. High ceilings. Crown molding. Rare hardwoods. To me it was just old. And gross. It cost me two bucks in fines the first time I saw it. And that was just from the outside.

Every wall had its share of cracks and holes. Layers of skeleton-white paint covered everything—door knobs, light fixtures, window frames. The musty smell reminded me of my grandma's.

Our previous house had been just the opposite. Three years new. Modern fixtures. The carpet smelled fresh. It would have qualified for the cover of *House Beautiful,* compared to House Dreadful where we now lived. At first, I complained to my parents nonstop. But that only made them upset, which made me feel worse. I didn't want to be mean. But it was so hard to say good-bye to the house I loved. It was even harder to say good-bye to my friends. Sarah and Katy were like sisters to me. We did everything together. Shared clothes. Spent the night. Ruled the school. Now they were half a state away. For the first time in my life, I knew how it felt to be lonely.

Kneeling at my dresser, I removed T-shirts from a box and put them in a drawer. Socks came next, followed by shorts. The humid air and eerie noises in the house started to get to me. I went to the living room to turn on the stereo, but the speakers weren't hooked up yet.

A bump on the outside of the house sounded like the garage door. What a relief. My dad was home from work—finally. I moved through the kitchen and pushed open the screen. It slammed behind me. "Dad?"

Our garage was a short ways from the house. The double door was already closed tight. I watched the side door, thinking my dad would walk out at any time. He didn't.

I stepped from the porch and jogged to the side of the garage. The doorknob wouldn't turn. I put my face against the square window. Something ran across it. I jumped back, repressing my urge to scream. A black widow paused on the inside corner of the glass, its red hourglass in plain view. It was creepy to think that so much poison was that close to my face. I forced myself to look past it. My dad's car wasn't there. I had definitely heard something, it just wasn't him.

But what was it?

Or who?

I walked backwards, keeping an eye on the garage door and the black widow. I scanned the perimeter of our yard. The bushes. The trees. Halfway back to the house, I felt them. Pointy feet on my shoulder. I screamed, slapped, and twisted—all at the same time. My heart raced. My lungs heaved. But there was no spider. Or web. Just a dry bush, thick with sharp twigs.

I took a deep breath and slowly exhaled. I was acting like a child, not a teenager. I hated spiders and bugs like every other girl my age—but I wasn't a baby. If I had to, I could flatten a spider like anyone.

Unless it was bigger than my foot . . .

I stopped in my tracks and stared at the wall. A spider's shadow moved toward the kitchen door. It was easily ten inches across. I couldn't get enough air. My heart revved up again. I grabbed the biggest stick I could find and veered around the porch. I kept my distance. The front door would work fine.

But as my angle changed, so did my perspective. A garden spider had spun its web between the porch light and the wall. The shadow threw me off. The real thing was no match for my stick. I thought of the spider in the tree that bit my brother. The one that ran across my hand.

Payback time.

I knocked the spider from the web. It scurried across the floor, but didn't get far. I brought the stick down hard. *Whomp. Whomp. Whomp.* The garden spider turned to mush.

An eerie protest mingled with the sound of the stick. A cry. Or whimper. I held still. The noise stopped. I searched the darkness. The trees and shrubs seemed to close in on me. I noticed something I hadn't before. Webs. Some like hammocks. Others like wheels. They covered the grass. Hung from trees. Webs of every shape and size. I couldn't see the spiders, but I knew they could see me. Multiple eyes. Watching. Waiting to attack.

Another cry. Faint. Eerie. Not human. I looked at the spider guts on my stick. I dropped the stick and grabbed the screen door handle. Locked. I swallowed hard and ran to the front door. Locked. I checked the sliding glass door around back. Locked. I returned to the patio, my hands shaking.

Another cry filled the night, followed by the tremor of something black in the bushes that bordered our yard.

Chapter 3

"Hey!" I shouted at the dark image. I had to show it I wasn't afraid. "Get out of there!"

The figure didn't move. I could see legs—at least four, maybe more.

"Hey! I'm talking to you!" I threatened, acting tough on the outside. Inside, I wanted to faint. I edged to the screen door, my eyes like rivets on the dark figure. What if it charged me? What if it had a thing for spiders and came for revenge. "You heard me. Get!"

"Are you talking to me?" a creepy voice asked. A hand grabbed my hair.

I screamed at the top of my lungs and wheeled around.

"Jaime, calm down," my dad said. He stood in the open screen door in a suit and tie. His keys were in his hand.

I clung to his chest and wouldn't let go. "It's out there!"

"What's out there?"

"I don't know. But it's there." I pointed at the bushes.

The image was gone.

That did it. Half talking, half sobbing, I told my dad everything. He brought me inside and waited for me to calm down. Then he turned on every light in the house. That helped. He asked me detailed questions about the spiders and Conner's bite.

"Now what?" I asked him. "Should we go to the hospital? Should we call?"

My dad shook his head. "First we should pray."

Of course. I should have thought of that long before now.

We bowed our heads. My dad prayed for Conner to be all right. He prayed for my mom and the rest of us. He prayed for all of the adjustments involved in moving to a new home.

The word "new" stuck in my head, even after he said amen. I tried to contain myself but couldn't. "If we had to move, why couldn't we buy a *new* house? This place is gr—"

My dad cleared his throat to keep me from saying it. "This house has hidden beauty, Jaime.

You'll see." He flopped the yellow pages on the kitchen table and started looking. "Here we are. You want to dial the hospital for me?"

I picked up the white cordless phone. I was still frustrated about our house. But there was nothing I could about it now. "What's the number?"

My dad read it to me.

I pushed the buttons, then brought the phone to my ear. Nothing. No dial tone. No ringing. It was dead. I offered the phone to my dad.

"That's strange," he said. "This was supposed to have been turned on by now. I thought your mom checked it."

"Me too," I said. I remembered the dark image in the bushes. The eerie cry. "Maybe someone cut the line."

My dad got up and faced the black kitchen window. "You're sure you saw someone out there?"

"Someone or *something,*" I said dismally.

He went to the screen door and poked his head outside. "There's nothing out here now."

I gasped when he brought his head back inside. "D-dad," I stuttered, pointing a shaky finger at his head. "Sp-spider!"

He lifted his eyes as though he could see the top of his own head. "Where?"

"Th-th-there!" I choked. A yellow spider set atop my dad's gray hair. Its belly was as round as a marble. Still trembling, I dug an iron skillet from one of the boxes. "Hold still, Dad."

"Calm down, Jaime," my dad told me. He acted more afraid of me than the spider.

I raised the iron skillet. "Don't worry, Dad. I'm getting good at this."

My dad gestured for me to stand back. Then he doubled over and shook his head. That didn't work. The spider held tight.

I moved in to take a swing. One smashed spider coming up.

My dad saw me coming. He swiped at his hair before I could help him. The spider landed on the hardwood floor and scurried for the cabinets. I sprang into action and took a swing with the iron skillet. *Thunk!*

"Jaime, stop it! You'll scar the floor." My dad took the frying pan away from me. The spider disappeared beneath the cabinets.

"Dad!" I moaned. "It got away."

My dad didn't care. He said he'd never seen a spider that yellow in his life. Like a sunflower. "It was probably rare, if not endangered." He couldn't get over the spider's striking color.

I could. Color didn't matter to me. Location did. Under a cabinet now. But where next? My bedroom? Would it nest in my hair when I went to sleep? That thing was gross. I didn't say it, but

I thought it. I never wanted to see it again. I moved to the center of the living room and sat on the carpet to sulk. My dad watched me for a moment, then came over. Before he could say anything, we heard something upstairs. I thought of the dark figure on the edge of our yard. Cutting the phone line was just the beginning; now it was coming for us.

I followed my dad up the creaky stairs. From room to room. He found something to admire at every turn. Carved moldings. Antique fixtures. A cherry wood window sill. He had forgotten *why* we had come upstairs in the first place. I was about to remind him when headlights flashed through one of the front windows. My mom and brother had come home. I said a "thank-you" prayer and hurried downstairs.

Conner strutted through the kitchen door. Mom followed and gave us the lowdown. The doctor didn't think Conner's bite was anything more than an allergic reaction. He'd put some medicine on it and a bandage. The swelling had gone down already. That only made Conner more determined to return to the tree house. He talked like it was the greatest thing on earth.

I focused on the deadly spiders. I described the one with the wall-to-wall web.

My mom cringed and got the shivers just hearing about it.

"You should have seen the yellow spider on Dad," I went on. "The one he let get away." I told my mom and Conner what happened.

My mom glared at my dad, then focused on the kitchen cabinets. "Way to go, dear."

"Spiders are part of life," my dad reasoned. He rubbed my mom's shoulders. She was like me. We liked things neat and nice. My dad consoled her. "If spiders are so bad, why did God make so many of them?"

"Exactly," Conner added. "They serve a purpose. As long as they stay off my tree house, I don't have a problem with them. But if they crowd my space . . ." He pretended to bring his finger down on a can of spray. "It's Raid time."

"Dad, you can't let him go back up there," I said. "Those spiders are giant. Deadly too. Raid won't cut it."

That got to my dad. He told us he'd grown up around here and had never seen anything like the spider I was describing, not to mention the one that landed on his head. "Maybe some research is in order. How about a trip to the library? It's not too far from here."

"THE LIBRARY!" Conner whined. "That's worse than school."

"Does that mean Conner can't go back to the tree?" I asked.

"I'd rather you check with the library first," Dad said. "I can drop you in the morning on the way to work. You can call your mom when you're ready to come home."

"I don't believe this," Conner complained. "I'm ready to build, not read some boring books."

"Better safe than sorry," my mom said.

"Yeah," I grinned. "Better safe than sorry."

"By the way, Jaime owes a dollar," Conner said before leaving. He grumbled all the way to his room.

I didn't mind paying. We had delayed our return to the tree house. That made me feel better. Safer. If only the feeling didn't fade so fast. I returned to my room and started unpacking boxes. It's amazing how once a scary thought gets in your head, it stays there. I couldn't reach into a box or grab a shoe without fearing that a spider would crawl out and latch onto my hand. I almost asked my dad for leather gloves, but I worried a spider would already be inside, waiting to pinch my skin. My mind played tricks on me. A clump of lint looked like a black widow. Some white thread on the dresser looked like a web. I had never been so paranoid in my life.

"Get a grip," I told myself. I arranged some knickknacks on my desk. Ceramic pig. Jewelry box. Wood cross. I put together my pen holder and read the verse inscribed in the glass base: *If God is for us, who can be against us?*

I grabbed a sock and polished the words. Romans 8:31. Then I positioned my desk lamp above the pen holder and turned on the light. After reading the verse out loud three times, I closed my eyes and said it by heart.

Good thing I did.

Chapter 4

The next morning, Dad dropped us off downtown. I was instantly sorry. The library reminded me of a gothic castle. "Where's the drawbridge?" I muttered. I waited at the stone steps. "And I thought our *house* was old. This place is gross."

"Pay up," Conner said, extending his hand. "If it wasn't for you, we wouldn't even be here."

We climbed the steps and pushed through the solid wood doors. The librarian watched us coming. Silver glasses magnified her eyes. A bun held every white hair in place.

"Got any books on spiders?" Conner blurted out. Kids at the reading tables looked up. "Sissy here thinks we're going to die."

"No, I don't," I said in my defense. I sent an eyebrow warning to my brother. "Stop being such a jerk." Then I smiled at the librarian. She didn't reciprocate. "Um . . . I just thought it would be good to read up on them."

"Who? Jerks?" she said. Still no smile.

"Um . . . no. Spiders." I told her a little about the tree house, thinking it would soften her. It didn't.

The librarian typed something on her computer, then looked toward a row of books. After another glance at the monitor, she wrote numbers on a square of scratch paper. "Try these."

I took the paper and headed in the direction the librarian indicated.

Conner followed. We crossed through rows of tables, following a worn stretch of red carpet. The numbers on the ends of the rows told us we were getting close.

"This is it," I said. I moved between the towering stacks filled with old hardbacks. I scanned faded covers of green, yellow, and blue. The numbers increased. Almost there.

"This better be worth it," Conner complained.

"Here," I pointed at the number. The title read, *On Death and Dying*. Not good. I felt weak at the knees.

"Definitely worth it," Conner laughed. He pulled the book from the shelf and waved it in my face. "Go ahead, Sis. Open it up. Learn what spiders do. Read it and weep."

I knocked the book from Conner's hands. "Stop it. You're giving me the heebie jeebies."

Conner returned the book to the shelf and reeled off titles. "How about, *Deader Than a Doornail,* or *Better Off Dead,* or *Death Becomes—*"

"Would you stop it!" I snapped. I checked every spine. Every title. Not a spider book in the bunch. Nothing but death. I double-checked my scratch paper. We returned to the librarian.

At first she ignored us.

I cleared my throat.

"Back so soon?" she finally said.

I slid the paper to her. "This number's wrong."

She looked at me over her glasses before checking the number. "You're sure?"

"I wanted a book on spiders. You sent us to the section on death."

"Hmm," she muttered, sounding bothered. She returned to her computer and tightened her lips. "I see what happened. Here, try these." She wrote down several numbers then pointed me in a different direction. We turned through aisles and rows. Right. Left. Right again. The numbers matched. We stepped into a narrow row of books just as someone fled the other end. I caught a glimpse of a dirty T-shirt and faded pants. Nothing more.

"Bummer," Conner grumbled. "She messed up again. This section says *Arachnids.*"

"Finally," I said.

"What do you mean, finally?" Conner asked.

"*Arachnid* is the scientific name for spider."

"It is?" Conner cleared his throat. "I mean, I know."

I ignored him and picked over the numbers to find the ones the librarian had given me. I muttered out loud, then stopped. The first title on the list was gone. I kept looking. The second book on the list? Gone. Third? Gone. So were the rest. I had never seen such a big gap on a library shelf in my life.

Only one book on spiders remained on the shelf, and it was ancient and torn. Dust caked the spine. "Gross."

Conner extended his palm. "Two bits, please."

I pulled a quarter from my pocket, then opened the book. It had hardly any pictures. The scientific names were impossible to pronounce.

"Oh, well," Conner conceded. "We gave it our best shot. I'll call Mom to come get us."

"Not yet," I told him. I knelt and kept looking. "How could so many spider books be gone? There's something not right about this."

"The only thing *not right* is the fact that we're here. I should be building that tree house. *My* tree house. Come on." Conner yanked my arm.

"Stop it," I snapped, shaking loose. "I'm going to keep looking. There's got to be something here."

Conner walked away, grumbling. "Suit yourself."

"Where are you going?" I asked.

"To get a book on tree houses. Find me when you're done. And hurry up."

I pulled another hardback from the shelf. It was dictionary-thick and filled with all sorts of technical mumbo jumbo. I read the words beneath a black and white sketch. "*Liphistitus desultor?*" I looked around like there should be someone to translate for me. There wasn't. I put the book back on the shelf and stood up. "Ah, forget it."

One row over, footsteps trailed away from me. I peered through the books but couldn't see anyone. *Weird,* I thought. Another disappearing character. I left the row in frustration. All I wanted was a book on poisonous spiders. From what I could tell, they had tons of spider books, but nearly all of them were gone. I decided on one last visit to the librarian before finding Conner.

She hadn't budged. I jumped into my explanation, but paused when I heard a commotion behind me. I turned to see two boys chasing a third boy down an aisle. The one on the run clutched a stack of books in his arms and kept his head down.

The librarian stood hastily to her feet. "Excuse me, young men!" she barked.

The two boys gave up their chase and disappeared into the magazine row. The librarian marched after them. Soon her angry voice filled the room. The bullies snickered, but not for long. When the librarian returned, she had the two of them by the shirt collars. She showed them the door, then returned to the counter. "You were saying?"

I stood in a daze. Speechless. Some town. I felt sorry for the boy with the books and myself at the same time. Would it be any different when I went to school, without friends to stick up for me? I looked around for Conner.

The librarian cleared her throat. "You were saying?"

"Um . . . the spider books you wrote down for me aren't there."

The librarian was all business. "Do you want me to put them on hold for you?"

"That's OK. I just wanted to learn about a huge spider I saw in a tree." I described it for her in vivid detail, thinking she might feel some sympathy for me.

Wrong again.

The librarian watched me with her magnified eyes. "Spiders are everywhere this time of year—especially around here. Some are deadly, you know."

"I know."

"There's an arachnid expert who comes in all the time. Perhaps he can help you." She slid me a pencil and scratch paper. "Write out what you told me."

I described the spider as best I could. The size and shape. The orange and black legs. The giant wheel of a web.

The librarian glanced at the note. "Where can I call you with his reply?"

I gave her our number. "The phone should be working by now. If not, just keep trying."

She added something to the note. "Fine. In the meantime, you might want to avoid that tree house."

No problem, I thought. *But try telling that to Conner.* I left the librarian to search for him. I started in the reference section. People sat at tables, caught up in their reading. A woman leafed through a gardening magazine. A college kid studied an encyclopedia. A boy with black hair hid his face behind a newspaper. He had a deformed hand. I didn't say "gross," but thought it, and felt guilty because of it.

Moving on, I checked the audio section and copier room. When Conner didn't turn up, I returned to the librarian. I asked her if there was such a thing as a book on building tree houses.

She gave me a number and title. It wasn't there. Neither was Conner. I searched adjacent aisles. Nothing. I went upstairs. Downstairs. I roamed every floor and department. No Conner. I decided to check the section of spider books again, just in case Conner went back there to look for me. He wasn't there. But I took a second to look at the books again in case I had missed one.

Breathing came from one row over. "Conner?"

I rounded the shelf. Deserted. A book fell in the row I was just in. I swallowed. "Conner, is that you?" I moved back to the spider section. Again, empty. I moved to the main aisle. No one in sight. The steps came again. Two rows down. I hurried there. Nothing. I held my breath and listened. It sounded like breathing one row over. I leaned forward and peered through an opening in the books. My nose brushed against the musty spines.

I saw a hand.

It jabbed through the opening and grabbed my face.

Chapter 5

My cheeks were still burning when my mom came. I was ticked at Conner for his lame prank. When he'd grabbed my face I had screamed, then felt stupid when people came running.

"I was just goofing off." Conner rolled his eyes and handed my mom the fifty cents he had collected from me. He told me he couldn't find any books on tree houses, so he went outside. That's why I couldn't find him. He wanted to brainstorm and thought looking at trees might do the trick.

Supposedly, it did. Once we got home, Conner called my dad to see if he could use the boards piled behind the garage. My dad was in a meeting, but his secretary promised to leave a message. Conner took that to mean yes. He rummaged through a big box in the garage for tools.

He found a hammer, level, and saw before getting distracted by an archery set. "I forgot I even had this," he announced. He set up an empty box in the backyard and in no time arrows were flying. But there was more yard than box. The grass stains on the arrows proved it.

When the mail came, I left Conner alone. Sarah and Katy said they'd write daily. But there was nothing for me. Not one letter.

My dad didn't call back until four. Conner had to do some talking, but finally got permission to return to the tree, even though we didn't learn anything at the library. He grabbed a hammer, nails, and as many boards as he could carry. He even conned me into carrying a rope and saw.

Ten minutes later, we were at the base of the magnolia tree. Conner started up with the rope and tools, moving fast.

I scanned the thick limbs and green leaves hanging above us. I still couldn't get over the tree's size. It was impossible to see through the dense foliage to the top. I wondered what was up there, and whether the eerie sounds would return. The spiders had come back with a vengeance. White silk hung everywhere, shaped like hammocks, nets, wheels, even funnels.

"Good thing you're not a fly," I yelled at Conner.

He pulled the hammer from his pouch and used the claw end to rip a web from the trunk. An orange spider scurried over the bark, but didn't get far. It had stout legs and a jelly bean for a body. Conner flattened it with one swing. He wiped the guts on his jeans. "That serves notice to the rest of the spiders not to mess with me."

"Yeah, sure," I said. "Now they'll want revenge."

Conner ignored me and climbed to the main house. From there he explored the other platforms, except for a few way up high. Then he returned to the main house and lowered the rope. "Start tying."

I grabbed some of the boards and tied them with the rope. "Go ahead."

Conner hoisted them up. We repeated the process until all of the boards were in the main house. "Get up here, Jaime. It's hammer time."

I stalled, then grabbed the first rung. Carefully, I followed the spiral steps to the main house. The huge spider from yesterday and its wall-to-wall web weren't there. At least not yet.

Conner quickly finished the rail on the view deck. "Now, for the family room." He pointed to a platform about ten feet above us that balanced on a thick, forked limb. It had one wall and no rails.

"Who says that's the family room?" I asked, tired of Conner's bossy attitude.

"Me."

"Then what's that one?" I pointed to a boxy little enclosure not far from the main house.

"That's the kitchen. You'll cook for me there."

"Funny." I glared at Conner, desperate for a comeback. When the shadow crossed his cheek, I had one. "I hope you like spider soup."

"Not again," Conner grumbled. A spotted spider clamped onto the end of his nose.

I squirmed and waved my hands in the air. "Gr—, I mean, sick!"

Conner crossed his eyes then took a swipe. He hit himself in the process. "Ouch."

"Did you get bit?"

He shook his head, still holding his nose.

"Are you sure? We'd better go home, just in case."

Conner assured me he didn't get bit and that we should get to work. He climbed to the family room and had me hand up boards. He measured and sawed and hammered. I made it my job to watch for spiders. They kept their distance, but I wondered for how long. They had us surrounded and outnumbered. A rusty garden spider spun a web. The strands of white silk stretched from center to edge in perfect proportion. I tried to admire it, but couldn't. All I could think about was a breeze blowing it in my face.

I closed my eyes and rubbed my temples. I went over the verse from my pen holder. "If God is for us, who can be against us." I repeated the words and asked the Lord to help me calm down. Conner wasn't the only one who liked tree houses. Normally, this place would be a dream. I prayed for selective vision. That helped. I opened my eyes with a better attitude.

Someone had definitely worked hard on this place. I counted several platforms in addition to the main house. Some were made of plywood. Others were made of pallets like you'd find behind a supermarket. One made the perfect lookout. It wrapped around a vertical limb up high. I pointed it out to Conner and suggested that we call it the crow's nest.

"Sure, whatever," he said, consumed with the project at hand.

The crow's nest appeared to have a complete view of our house. Too bad it didn't have rails or walls of any kind. I couldn't imagine standing on the platform without hugging the tree for dear life.

The strangest sight was near the top of the tree. A cluster of branches and leaves partially concealed a small deck. At least I think that's what it was. Twigs twisted together to form the bottom and sides. The limb that held it went straight up and down like a lamp post. But there was nothing to climb on. No ladder. No branches.

In another case, a plank led from one room of the tree town to another, then just stopped in midair. Another unfinished project had a roof but no floor. Figuring out what the original builder had in mind was like looking at a partially finished jigsaw puzzle—with no box top picture to go by.

Conner pounded away. He was having fun and didn't care about the tree's mysterious history. But I did. I wanted answers. I eyed an upper platform and decided to go for it. It was above where Conner was working. It had thick rails. I climbed past Conner and kept going.

"Hey watch it," he told me.

"What? I didn't do anything."

"You knocked something down on my head."

"No I didn't."

"Well, something hit me."

I paused on the limb, not sure I wanted to go any higher. I looked at the platform. No spiders in sight. I stepped on a Y in the limb and grabbed a branch. I climbed higher. Something bumped my back. "Stop it."

"Stop what?" Conner asked.

"You threw something at me."

"No, I didn't." He hammered some more.

A branch creaked above me. I remembered my first visit here. What was up there? I snapped loose a twig and tossed it at the platform. Nothing happened. I eased higher. My legs began to shake. My hands started to sweat. "Conner, you want to check out this platform for me?"

"I already did," he said.

"You're sure?"

"Sure."

I climbed higher. Another bump. I scanned the upper branches. Nothing in sight. No one. I reached above me and grabbed the platform. I pulled myself up.

One look at the floor and I started screaming.

Chapter 6

Bloody guts littered the floor, covered with flies. "GA-ROSS!"

"Now what?" Conner asked. He sounded irritated.

I lowered myself to the family room. "Sick."

Conner returned to his hammering.

"There's something dead up there!" I told him.

"What, a mouse?"

"Bigger."

"A squirrel?"

I caught his hammer at the top of his swing. "Bigger."

Conner muttered something about another quarter and that I was being a baby, but finally agreed to check it out. His response made me feel better. "Gross."

"I told you."

He started down, then paused halfway. "Hand me that board."

I handed up the short piece of wood from the family room. "You said you checked that platform."

"I did."

Our necks doubled back as we searched the upper branches.

"I told you we shouldn't have come here," I told him.

Conner eyed the guts. There was blood and fur. "It's probably a rabbit. A hawk must have dropped it."

I didn't buy Conner's hawk theory. We hadn't seen a bird in the tree since we arrived. There was no sign of a nest. No feathers, bird doo-doo, anything.

"I know what killed it," I informed him. "A spider."

"Sure. A spider. The world's biggest grand-daddy longlegs." Conner used the board to scrape the remains from the platform.

I watched them disappear over the edge and fall beneath the tree. Tall weeds pushing through the dead leaves and stones concealed where the mess landed. For some reason I thought about falling. I calculated where I would hit the ground. How much it would hurt. Sharp rocks waited in all the wrong places. My hands tightened around a branch and I returned my attention to Conner. But an image flickered in the corner of my eye. I looked down again. I scanned the leaves and stones until I found it. Weeds did their best to hide it, but couldn't. It was there, lying flat. A cross.

Two limbs rested on the ground, cut to the right length. The shorter one fit on top of the longer one. They were as thick as a man's leg and gray from the weather.

I pointed at the cross. "Conner, look!"

He pushed the last bit of guts over the edge before looking where I was pointing. "Weird."

"You want to check it out?" I asked.

When he didn't answer me right away, I expected him to pick up his hammer and get back to work. But he didn't. He just stared at the cross. "I guess. If you do."

"Let's go." We climbed down and stomped through the overgrowth. I took a roundabout way to avoid the guts. Conner followed. As we neared the cross, I nearly tripped over a stone. A closer look revealed a circle of stones that wrapped around the entire cross. The tall weeds hid them from view, but they were there. We stepped inside the circle to view the cross. We put our hands on our knees and bent over. The ends of each limb had been cut with a saw. Notches where the two limbs came together allowed the top piece to fit perfectly flush with the bottom.

"Is that a name?" Conner asked. He pointed at the short section of the cross.

I squatted and peered closer but still couldn't tell. I brushed debris and dry grass from the letters carved into the wood. "I think so. This is definitely a *D*."

"And that's an *H*," Conner added.

I blew along the horizontal beam, hitting every crevice and hole. I got so close my lips almost brushed the smooth surface of the cross. The mulch and dirt scattered. That made the difference.

"It is a name," Conner admitted. "With two numbers."

I underlined the letters as I read. "D-E-A-N H-I-L-T-O-N. Dean Hilton?" The numbers given appeared to be years, with a difference of fifteen between them.

We searched the cross for more carvings, but couldn't find any. That didn't matter. We both had a pretty good idea of what we had found.

"Do you think Dean died in a fall?" I asked.

"Probably," Conner admitted. "Why else would this be here?"

Instinctively, we both looked up. We scanned the tree for evidence, for something to connect what was above with the memorial at our feet.

"He could have fallen from anywhere," I suggested.

"Could have," Conner said. "Maybe he's buried here, just a foot deep, ready to reach out and get you."

"Knock it off," I said. "What if he is?"

"What if?" Conner bulged his eyes and grabbed my ankle, trying to freak me out.

I stood and twisted away.

He followed, his hands like claws. I stumbled and tripped. He kept coming. He spoke like a zombie. "Dean wants revenge."

I backed toward the trunk of the giant tree. "Knock it off. You're giving me the creeps."

Conner moaned and made his eyes wild. He would have kept coming, except for one thing.

A spider stopped him. It landed on his bare arm.

One dropped on me too—on my head. Another followed. It stuck to my shoulders. Spiders rained down like hail. Small ones. Big ones. Black. Gray. Green.

I shrieked and twisted. Conner shouted and slapped. But it wasn't enough. The spiders kept falling.

Chapter 7

"RUN!" Conner shouted.

I bolted from the tree, slapping myself silly. I started to scream, but a spider fell in my mouth. I spit it out and wiped my lips. "GROSS-SS!"

Conner passed me in a full sprint. He made it to a grass field and rolled. He struck his arms, face, his whole body. Then he took off his shirt and used it like a whip. He snapped his back and legs.

I rolled next to Conner. He used his shirt on my arms until all the spiders were gone.

"Are you all right?" he asked.

I stood, my heart pounding. My skin sweaty. I took deep breaths. "I think so."

"Me too," he said.

We kept searching our clothes. The spiders were gone. We waited for the stinging sensation.

With that many spiders, bites were inevitable. Poisonous bites. But the pain never came.

"I can't believe we didn't get bit," I told him.

Conner rubbed his neck, then checked his hand, as if it should be dotted with blood. It wasn't. He checked his arms. No bites.

"Now what?" I asked.

Before Conner could answer, we saw something move in the upper branches. We had run too far from the tree to see what it was. But there was something there. Something brown and leggy, the size of a bear cub. It dropped from an upper branch to a lower limb without a sound. It scurried along the bark, then disappeared behind a cluster of leaves.

"What was that?" I muttered, my eyes fixed on the tree.

Conner looked at the tree for a long time . . . but didn't say a word.

That night, Conner used the tools we'd left behind as a bargaining chip. "We can't just leave them there to rust. Come on, Dad."

My dad gave in. He had a thing about tools lasting for generations.

My mom didn't. After hearing about the spiders, the cross, and the mysterious creature, she didn't want us anywhere near the tree.

"We didn't get bit," Conner whined. "We're fine. Besides, tomorrow I'll take a can of Raid. Make that two cans."

"Raid won't stop that animal you saw, whatever it was." My mom looked at me, knowing I would agree.

I nodded, but didn't say anything. As much as the tree scared me, I sort of wanted to return. The mystery of it all intrigued me. I wanted to know what happened there. And why.

The phone startled us. My dad answered. "Hello?"

We watched him as he listened.

"It's for you, Jaime," he said. "A librarian?" He tossed me the cordless receiver.

I greeted the librarian with guarded anticipation. She told me that the spider expert had come by and written a response to my description. He offered a probable name and other information that might be helpful.

"Can you read it to me?" I asked.

"It's rather long," she told me. "You can pick it up tomorrow."

I hung up and relayed the information to my family.

"Sounds like a great idea," my mom said. "You two can ride your bikes there first thing in the morning."

I gave my mom a look. "Ride our bikes?"

"Afraid so. I'll be attending a women's Bible study."

"Not the library again," Conner moaned. "I want to work on the tree house."

"You should go to the library first," my mom said. "Better to play it safe. Learn what you can. If everything checks out, you can work on the tree house later."

Conner grumbled for a while, then gave in. He found some paper and drew a diagram of the tree house. My parents wanted to see it after hearing so much about it. The drawing helped me too. The tree house really did have incredible potential. And since Conner and I hadn't met any friends, it was something to do until school started. When we did make friends, we could all hang out there.

I went to my room to finish unpacking. I had clothes to put away still. Books too. I dug them from the box and placed them on the shelf. When I got to my yearbook, I paused. Seeing it made me think of the friends I had left behind. Maybe their letters would come tomorrow. I read the inscriptions on the inside cover. I flipped through the pages to see their faces again. Sarah. Katy. Denise. Marco was such a pest, but he made me laugh. A tear ran down my cheek and onto the page, causing it to warp.

"We rule this school," I whispered, remembering our saying. It wasn't a mean thing. We didn't pick on anyone. Kids just wanted to be with us.

I flipped through the pages, appreciating faces. Then a name caught my eye. Dean Tomkins. He was the school's star skateboarder. But it was his name that grabbed me. I thought of the cross beneath the tree. If Dean Hilton really died at age fifteen a few years ago, his picture would be in a high school yearbook. The town only had two high schools. I could check the library. If his picture appeared in last year's yearbook, then the year carved on the cross wasn't when he died.

I moved to my window and stared at the magnolia tree. It loomed above the grove with dark intent. In my mind, there was no doubt. The cross was Dean's memorial. The tree had taken his life at fifteen. The same age as Conner. I wondered if Dean had acted the same way, afraid of nothing, reckless.

BOOM!

An explosion of glass filled my room. I covered my face and fell away from the window.

I heard voices. Shouting.

The sound of running feet.

I peered through my fingers.

Chunks of glass covered the floor. A loose piece fell from the window and shattered.

Then I saw it. Next to me.

An arrow stained with dirt and grass.

Chapter 8

We pulled our bikes from the garage after breakfast and started for the library. I felt dead tired. Thanks to Conner's wild arrow, I went to bed with a broken window. Duct tape and a piece of cardboard marked "utensils" covered the hole. I hardly got any sleep, not with the tree of spiders looming in the distance. For some reason, glass seemed more capable of sealing out spiders than cardboard and tape.

My dad had already left for work. Conner peddled in front of me like always. He had a thing about leading. After we'd ridden a short ways, my mom drove past us enroute to her Bible study. Conner was watching the magnolia tree more than the road. He bounced through a pothole and nearly wiped out.

"Nice one," I told him.

Conner slowed down, oblivious to everything but the tree.

Soon, I passed him. He didn't say anything or try to regain the lead. He just watched the tree. It was a hundred yards away, across a field. I had a feeling I knew what he was thinking. "Don't get any ideas."

"About what?"

"You know." I slowed down and positioned my bike between him and the tree. That wasn't enough.

"Why don't you go to the library without me?" Conner suggested, trying to sound innocent. "It doesn't take two of us to read a note."

"But Mom said you had to go with me."

"No, she didn't."

"Yes, she did."

"She said it was a good idea. That's all. Maybe it's a better idea for me to build the tree house while you go to the library." Conner didn't wait for my comeback. He hit his brakes and skidded. By the time I stopped, he had hopped the curb and was starting across the field.

I yelled at him to come back, but he didn't. I threatened to tell. Conner ignored me. He peddled over dirt clods and dry brush, his sights set on the town in the sky. There was no point in going after him. Once he got an idea in his head, forget it.

I started for the library again, picking up speed. I wanted to read the note and get back pronto. The thought of Conner working alone in the tree, surrounded by deadly spiders, scared me. I rode up a hill, then down. The morning air smelled of sprinklers and exhaust. I passed old stores with wooden signs. My wheels vibrated over brick streets and cracked sidewalks. By the time I reached the library, my legs burned. I locked my bike and climbed the stone steps. I went for the drinking fountain first, then to the reference desk.

A woman with shiny red hair watched me approach. "Can I help you?"

I told her about the note.

She checked a few shelves and drawers. "I don't see anything with your name on it." She held her chin and glanced around. "Hmm." She leafed through a stack of papers, then looked under a book. "Sorry."

"But the librarian called me at home. She said she had something for me."

The woman checked her watch. "She'll be here in about thirty minutes."

"Okay," I said, feeling frustrated. "I can wait." I stood there trying to think of what to do. Then I remembered my other objective. I asked her if they had yearbooks from the local high schools and where could I find them?

"Yearbooks, huh?" She thought for a moment then pointed down an aisle.

I hurried away, passing the same assortment of people I had seen the day before: Kids with glasses and extra pencils, men reading business newspapers and punching numbers into their calculators, boys paging through picture books. No one even noticed me. That would never have happened where I used to live. People knew me. They smiled and said hello. Not here.

I found the yearbooks on the bottom shelf in the middle of the row. I knelt and scanned the years. I started with Central High three years back. I mumbled names from the sophomore class. "Greg Harris. Mark Hikleman. Joanne Hinson." I double checked. No Dean Hilton. I checked the juniors, then freshmen. Dean Hilton never appeared. I repeated the process with the yearbook from two years ago. Same results. I tried last year's yearbook but didn't do any better. So much for Central High. That left Royal Oak High. This time I started with the sophomore class from two years ago.

"Joshua Henry. Nadine Hill. Dean . . ." My finger stopped on the small black and white photo. Oval face. Dark hair. Fair skin. The name matched. It was him. Dean Hilton. I found myself staring at his picture, trying to imagine what he had been like. Had he built the tree house alone, or with friends? Did the cross really mark his death?

I put the yearbook away and grabbed the following year. I took my time, in no rush to confirm what I already feared. The blue cover said Royal Oak Romans. I let out a breath and looked around. I listened for breathing. Nothing. I was alone.

I opened the yearbook and turned the glossy pages to the junior class, Dean's grade for that year. The faces were familiar. Joshua Henry. Nadine Hill. David Hilts. I stared at the row of black and white faces and names. Dean Hilton was gone. I double checked the alphabetical order. I flipped pages. Same result. I turned to the sophomore class just in case he flunked and didn't advance. He wasn't there.

Dean Hilton was gone.

I had to tell Conner.

I checked my watch. It had only been ten minutes. The librarian wasn't due for another twenty. I strolled back to the information counter anyway, just in case she'd come to work early. She hadn't. Not only that, the other lady was gone. I stood at the counter and glanced around. On the desk behind the counter, Post-It notes buried the phone. A stack of files filled a basket. The top one caught my eye. It looked like it had my name on it.

The people at the reading tables were consumed with their papers and books. I checked my watch. Eighteen more minutes. The other librarian was still gone. I thought about Conner in the tree alone. I thought about Dean Hilton and the memorial cross. I thought about the spiders. That did it. I couldn't wait any longer. Keeping an eye on the readers, I pushed open the half-door to the librarian's desk. I was wrong about the folder. It had someone else's name on it. I started to leave, then noticed a paper like the one I had left the note on. A thick reference book covered half of it. I moved the book aside and picked up the paper.

That's when the hand grabbed me.

"What are you doing?" a shrill voice asked.

I spun around, breathless.

The white-haired librarian towered over me, her eyes hard, her bun tight. She snatched the paper from my hand. "You're not allowed back here."

"I'm sorry. It's just that I knew there was a note for me and you still hadn't come and my brother went to the tree and . . ." I babbled away until she finally cut me off.

"OUT!" She put her hand on my back and pushed me to the other side of the counter. When

I noticed everyone watching, I wanted to hide. My face burned, beet red.

"Sorry," I said again.

The librarian pulled a sheet of notebook paper from one of her file trays. "Here's what you're looking for. Sounds to me like advice worth heeding. Mr. Scopula is quite the expert on arachnids."

I unfolded the piece of paper and started reading.

> Jaime,
>
> The spider you've described is the *Nephila Inaurata* or Giant Orb Weaver. Unique characteristics include bands of orange and black on the legs and a cone shaped abdomen. The webs measure up to seven feet across. The silk is yellow and strong, capable of catching small birds as prey. Their venom is deadly. Take my advice, *avoid the* Nephila *at all cost.* Orb spiders are fast and aggressive. If one bites you, you will die.
>
> Mr. Scopula

The last line made me weak. I looked up at the librarian. She stared back, her face hard. I hid behind the note and re-read the words, especially the last line. I had a gut feeling someone was watching me, but not the librarian. I heard a rustling at the reading tables. I turned. No one acknowledged me. Everyone was in his own world, while mine was crashing down. I stuffed the note in my pocket and sprinted for the exit. The librarian yelled after me to slow down, but I didn't. All I could think about was the deadly spider lying in wait for my brother.

Chapter 9

"Conner!" I shouted. I peddled to the base of the tree and threw my bike down. I cupped my hands and yelled into the forest above. "Conner!" He didn't answer. I circled the massive trunk, but couldn't see him. I had thought about the Giant Orb spider the whole way over. Had it already bit Conner? Was Conner lying on one of the platforms, dead?

I grabbed the first slat and started up. I climbed hand over hand around the trunk. At the main house, I carefully poked my head inside. "Conner?"

He wasn't there.

Neither was the giant web. I climbed inside, then went to the view deck. I searched the upper branches, but couldn't see him. Next stop, family room. No Conner. No deadly Orb spider. But plenty of others had moved in. One had a web in the corner that looked like a funnel. A spider with furry legs clung to the wall. I kept climbing. I checked another platform. Then another. I started across a rope bridge that connected two rooms, but decided against it. Too many spiders guarded the way.

I returned to the deck of the main house, covered with dust and leaves and cobwebs. "Conner?" I said it more as a question than a demand. I searched the upper reaches of the tree. My eyes came to rest on the highest platform, the one made of branches bound together. The widow's watch. Conner would have had to shinny twenty feet to get there. He could have done it, maybe. But had he?

I cupped my hands again and shouted the note's contents at the tree top. I waited for movement, for Conner to stick his head over the edge and say something smart like, "What kept you?" But he didn't.

Then something occurred to me. What if Conner was up there, but unable to speak? What if he'd found a dozen Giant Orb spiders waiting? I thought of the guts we found yesterday. Were they the remains of a spider's feeding frenzy?

I wiped the sweat from my face. It was all I could do not to climb down and run straight home. But I couldn't leave my brother. I said a prayer for God's protection. I quoted my verse, "If God is for us, who can be against us?"

I started up. I scaled the main trunk before veering to the limb that held the widow's watch. I thought my heart would overheat. It told me to stop. So did common sense. But I had to try. When I ran out of branches to step on, I began to worm my way up. I squeezed the bark with my legs, and stretched my arms. Then I hugged the tree with my arms, and lifted my legs. I felt like an islander climbing a palm tree. Little by little I edged higher.

Only ten more feet to the widow's watch. But I needed a break. I paused to catch my breath. My tongue was sticky. Cotton mouth. Thirst. My arms were raw from hugging the tree. So were my legs.

Just as I started again, something touched my ankle.

I flinched, barely. It climbed onto my skin. I couldn't loosen my hold enough to see it. Its legs felt light and sharp. The front feet prodded my skin, testing it, then continued to climb. I wanted to scream, to reach down and flatten it. But I couldn't let go. And I didn't dare move.

I pictured the Giant Orb spider in my mind and the note left by Mr. Scopula. His warning haunted me. "Avoid the *Nephila* at all cost . . . or you will die."

I held my breath. My T-shirt had slid up to expose the small of my back. The spider walked across it. I hoped it couldn't smell fear. I squeezed the tree with all my might. I pressed my face into the bark and whimpered.

The spider climbed onto my shoulder. At first sight of the legs, I muffled a cry. A tear ran along my nose. It was the *Nephila,* the Giant Orb Weaver. It moved closer to my face. Closer.

I couldn't bear to watch. The fangs would come next, sinking into my neck or temple. I prayed like never before. For strength. For stamina. For life. "If God is for us," I whispered. I decided those words would be my last. If I died mid-sentence, I'd finish the verse in heaven. I whispered the words again and again. Then the Giant Orb stepped from my shoulder.

I almost opened my eyes, thinking relief.

That's not what I found. The *Nephila* stared back at me, less than an inch away. Its fangs pinched together, ready to inject their venom. Its black and orange legs silently held the bark. All eight of its eyes held mine.

A frantic whimper escaped me. The Giant Orb stepped forward and lifted two legs as if to strike. I closed my eyes again, praying, and saying my verse, and preparing for death. But it never came. After a minute or two, I peeked through a slit in my eyelid. No *Nephila.* I opened my eyes all the way. The spider was gone.

I searched above. Gone. I scanned further up the tree. Along the branch. No Giant Orb Weaver. But something else caught my eye. A round outline on the limb. A branch had been there. The size looked familiar. I spotted the letters next, the initials D. H.

Instinctively, I looked down. I searched for the cross in the tall grass. It was there. Then another image registered in the corner of my eye. The blue shirt. The back of a head. He was hidden by a bush and overgrown weeds, but there was no mistaking the clothes and still body of my brother.

Chapter 10

"Conner!" I screamed.

I slid down the limb, scraping my legs and arms. I reached a branch and dropped to the next. My body shook. I wanted to cry, but didn't. "Conner?"

He didn't move.

I jumped to the deck of the main house and rushed inside. I dropped through the hatch in the floor. My feet dangled in midair before finding a wood slat. I took the rungs two at a time. Five feet from the ground, I let go. I hurdled weeds and bushes to get to Conner. I fell to my knees. He was lying on his stomach with his face in the grass. I nudged his shoulder and begged. "Conner, wake up."

He didn't.

I examined him from head to toe, not sure what to do. If the Giant Orb Weaver had bitten him, there was nothing I could do. Nothing anyone could do. I placed my hands on his back and prayed. At first nothing happened. Then I felt the subtle rise of his back. He was breathing. He was alive.

I brought my lips to his ear. "Conner, wake up. It's me. Jaime." I shook his arm and kept talking.

Pretty soon he muttered. Then his eyes flickered and he looked at me.

"Conner, what happened? Are you all right?"

"Um . . . I don't know," Conner mumbled. He rolled on his side, then to his back. He blinked quickly to get his bearings. "I guess I fell asleep."

Tears of joy filled my eyes. "Here?"

"I sort of spilled some nails when I was working on a platform." He sat up.

"Sort of?"

Conner wiped grass from his face. "Anyway, I came here to dig them out of the weeds. It took a while and I got tired." He looked around for the box. "What'd you do with them?"

"Nothing." I helped him look for the box of nails. "Maybe you fell from a platform and the nails are still up there."

"Sure." Conner stood up and kicked at the weeds. "The box was right here. I filled it nail by nail."

I searched the base of the tree. Nothing stirred. "Let's get out of here."

Conner positioned himself beneath the platform he had last worked on. "It was *right here*." He dug through the weeds and found a nail. "See?"

I just shook my head. "Something's not right about—"

"Don't start," Conner told me. "Wait until you see how much I got done." His tired legs staggered for the trunk of the tree. He acted like he fell or something bit him, one of the two.

I rushed in front of him and guarded the spiral ladder. "Forget it. You're not going back up there."

"I'm okay. I'm just tired." Conner put his hand on my shoulder, as if to push me aside. But he didn't try. He leaned on me for support.

That was my chance to tell him about the note.

"Poisonous, huh?" Conner brought his head back slowly and scanned the treehouse. "That's not the end of the world. Black widows are poisonous. But we still go in the garage."

"But these spiders are deadly. There's no cure."

Conner let the trunk hold him up. "That's just one guy's opinion. How does he know?"

"You want proof?" I pointed toward the cross. "Dean Hilton took his last picture as a sophomore. The next year, he was gone."

Conner didn't argue. He just let go of the rungs and stumbled to the circle of rocks that surrounded the cross.

I met him there. I told him about the yearbooks and how Dean disappeared.

"It's like I said before," Conner eventually said. "Pesticides. Next time we come here, we'll give the poisonous spiders a taste of their own medicine."

"But what if that doesn't work?" I asked. As much as I wanted to finish the tree house, if I never saw another spider again, it would be too soon. "What if one of the Giant Orb Weavers gets to you? Or me? What if you fall? We shouldn't be here, Conner. The tree is cursed."

"Cursed?" Conner said it slow, with emphasis. He looked at me like I was losing it. "Jaime, get a grip. It's not cursed. There's nothing that a few cans of pesticide won't fix. Raid, Jaime. That's all you need to know."

"Dead, Conner. That's all *you* need to know."

We argued for a while, but Conner wouldn't change his mind. "If we don't kill the spiders, who will? How would you feel if another kid died in this tree? If the Giant Orbs are so dangerous, let's do something about it."

I let out a breath, frustrated. Conner had a point.

Instead of riding our bikes across the rough terrain, we walked them. Conner still seemed a little dizzy. We found ourselves looking back constantly.

That's when I noticed something dark jump behind one of the elm trees near the magnolia.

"Did you see that?" I asked.

"I'm not sure what I saw." Conner clamped down his eyelids, then opened them. He raised his forehead as far as it would go.

"There was something there," I said.

"Here we go again," Conner muttered. He put down his bike. "Let's check it out."

Conner took the lead, veering to the right. I approached to the left of the tree. After a silent three count, we pounced.

"Got ya!" we blurted out. We swept around the trunk. Nothing was there.

We looked up, but couldn't find anything. The elm's branches mingled with an oak tree on one side. The oak reached across to the magnolia tree.

My eyes jumped from branch to limb, pausing at each bough and crevice, watching for movement.

"It was probably just a squirrel," Conner shrugged.

"It was bigger than that," I said. I kept my attention on the trees. I walked from one to the next.

Conner waited for me. "Well?"

I did a three-sixty with my neck doubled back. Nothing. "This whole grove is haunted."

"First cursed, now haunted," Conner laughed. "Reality check. It's not haunted. It's infested. Like I said, just give me a can of Raid."

A second later, that's exactly what dropped from the sky.

Chapter 11

I picked up the can and looked it over. Something had ripped open one side. Rust covered the dirty metal.

"Weird," Conner said. He searched the tree next to us. So did I. We took cautious steps, ready to defend ourselves if something else fell. Before long, our necks started to hurt from looking up.

"What were you saying about Raid?" I asked.

"Coincidence," Conner said. He searched for a way to climb the oak, but couldn't find one. When nothing else stirred, we headed home.

It's funny how one object can symbolize two completely different things, depending on who you ask. Conner saw the bug spray can as a sign that he was on the right track. Not me. I saw it as a sign that bug spray had been tried before and was no match for what was up there.

My mom took my side—at least initially. She had a fit when she learned Conner had gone to the tree instead of the library. Hearing about his nap and the disappearing nails only added fuel to her fire. "From now on, that tree is off-limits."

"But Mom," Conner protested.

"No buts about it," my mom told him.

I stood beside my mom, feeling relieved but disappointed too. Not only did I want Conner to finish the tree house, there was also a mystery that I wanted to solve. It was starting to get to me.

Conner wouldn't give up. He started in about the extreme danger to other kids in the neighborhood and how it was our responsibility to do something.

At first my mom wouldn't budge, but then she started to soften.

Conner could see it. He told her that if we went to the Home Warehouse store for pesticides, she could buy the mini-blinds she had been wanting. "A good pesticide would sure come in handy around this old house," Conner said, kicking into salesman mode. "The bugs around here are . . . what's the G word, Jaime?"

"Forget it," I told him. "I'm broke."

"Hmm," my mom said, thinking it over. "Bug spray would come in handy. And we do need blinds for the den."

"Exactly," Conner agreed.

My mom eyed him. "Don't get ahead of yourself, young man. You're not going anywhere near that tree until you talk to your dad."

Conner looked at his watch. "Fine with me. By the time we get back, he should be home from work."

My mom grabbed her purse and keys. We piled in the car and took off. My mom's attitude improved in a hurry. She loved to decorate. Choosing between unpacking and buying something new for the house was easy.

Conner sat in the front seat, full of himself. He sang with the radio and kept time on the dash. When my mom parked in front of the Home Warehouse, Conner jumped out first. We followed. On the way in, I noticed a bookstore sandwiched between a pharmacy and a flower shop. That gave me an idea.

I told Mom where I was going and that I'd catch up with them.

The bookstore was long and narrow and empty. In fact, I didn't even see any employees. I weaved through the rows until I found the section on nature. Books on pets dominated the shelf; dogs mostly, but cats and birds too. I scanned the titles, ready to give up. Then I found it. *A Field Guide to Spiders*.

I pulled it from the shelf and searched for the Giant Orb Weaver. It was there, the *Nephila.* Long legs, bands of orange and black. Huge web. Mr. Scopula's information checked out. Or did it? There was nothing mentioned about Giant Orbs being poisonous to humans. I re-read the page. It was definitely the right spider. But it wasn't deadly to humans.

I sat down and hid my face in the open book. I read about other Giant Orb spiders. Some were silver and black. All had long legs. But none was described as deadly to humans. I didn't get it. How could Mr. Scopula make such an obvious mistake? And if it wasn't a mistake, why did he lie to me?

"Not you again," a stern voice grumbled. A man came around the end of the shelf and crossed his arms. His name tag said Sid, with Manager above it. When I lowered the book, his angry expression faded. "You're not him."

I stood up, still holding the field guide. "Who?"

"A kid used to come in here and camp out." He pointed to the spot of carpet I occupied. "If I didn't run him off, he'd stay for hours."

"What would he read?" I asked.

"Same as you. Spider books. He took notes, read from cover to cover."

"Hmm . . ." I offered, at a loss for words.

The manager took that to mean that I wanted him to tell me more. "He'd crease the hardback bindings. Wear out the pages. Time he was done, I couldn't sell the books as new. You're not like him, are you?"

I shook my head. Sid returned to the register. I turned a few more pages, but this time with extra care. I couldn't believe the variety of spiders. On any other creature, the bright colors would have been beautiful. Too bad God wasted them on spiders.

"Jaime, what happened to catching up with us?" my mom asked, walking toward me.

"I guess I lost track of time," I told her. "By the way, can I get this?"

My mom couldn't believe I wanted to buy a book on spiders. "You're sure you want it?"

I nodded. "Better safe than sorry."

She checked the price, then carried it to the counter. "Wait till you see the blinds I bought. We also ordered you a new window. Your father can install it this weekend."

"I guess you're not like that kid after all," the manager said.

"What kid?" my mom asked.

I filled her in, then turned my attention to the manager. "What'd he look like, anyway?"

"He was a small kid. Quiet. He had straight black hair. Pale face." The man shrugged. "That's about it."

"When was he here last?" I asked.

The manager rang up my purchase. "It's been about six months, give or take. That'll be fourteen dollars and seventy-three cents."

My mom paid him.

"Do you remember his name?" I asked.

He looked at me. "You're full of questions, aren't you."

"It's just that I'm trying to learn about spiders and thought maybe he could help."

"Probably could. Just don't let him near your new book." The manager grinned. "He told me his name, but it's been too long. Sorry."

My mom headed for the door with her change. I followed, then turned around. I had to ask. The boy's description was too close to what I had seen in the yearbook. "Would you know his name if you heard it?"

"Probably," the manager said.

"Dean Hilton." I watched for a reaction.

The manager rubbed his chin, then snapped his fingers. "Yep. That's it. Dean Hilton. That was his name."

I shuffled outside in a daze. If Dean didn't die, where did he go? And why was there a memorial cross with his name on it under the magnolia tree?

Chapter 12

"Would you forget about Dean Hilton?" Conner groused. "The guy probably moved." We left the house armed with pesticides. Knowing the Giant Orb Weaver wasn't poisonous bolstered Conner's confidence. "That's what you get for listening to an *expert* you've never met."

"Maybe Mr. Scopula had a good reason for warning us to stay away," I reasoned. "Something's not right about that tree. You know it."

If he did, Conner wouldn't admit it. My mom just wanted us to be careful. Dad just wanted his tools back. He looked up the *Nephila* in my field guide, then practically shoved us out the door. "Don't forget! Tools!"

Dusk seemed like the best time to return to the tree. Even I knew spiders came out then. They'd spin their webs and wait. Insects would get caught. The spiders would move in for the kill.

The night was sticky. My shirt clung to my back. The spray can slid in my sweaty hand. I decided to hold it with both. Conner had brought a one gallon jug for himself and kept it in his backpack. A white plastic tube led to the spray trigger in his hand. Conner set the nozzle to shoot a pinpoint line, like a laser. As we hiked along, he practiced by blasting anything that moved.

"Quit wasting it," I told him. I had yet to use my can of Raid, determined to conserve it.

We paused beneath the magnolia tree long enough for Conner to put his trigger in the make-shift holster he had strapped to his waist. I put the spray can in his backpack. He promised to give it back once we reached the main house. Conner climbed the rungs, spiraling around the tree. He stopped half-way up, drew his spray trigger, and fired a few squirts. Then he reholstered the trigger and started again.

"What'd you shoot?" I asked.

"Mosquito." Conner reached the door beneath the main house and poked his head inside. He held a hand over his holster, but didn't grab the spray trigger. After a look around, he climbed all the way in. That surprised me. I thought for sure he'd have to shoot a spider or two. Maybe even the Giant Orb Weaver.

I hurried up the spiral ladder and joined Conner in the main house. "Where are the spiders?" I dug my can of Raid from the backpack.

Conner smacked his gum and looked around. "Hiding."

We moved to the view deck and went over our strategy. It was decided that I would take the kitchen and the platforms above it. Conner would hit the family room, crow's nest, and everything in between. We would converge near the tree top. If possible, Conner would go for the widow's watch.

He was still talking when something moved on the edge of my peripheral vision. I turned. A brown rope swayed back and forth. It was tied to an upper branch.

"Where'd that come from?" I asked.

"It's always been there."

"You sure?"

"Of course, I'm sure," Conner said. "I think."

"Why is it swaying?"

"The breeze."

"But there isn't a breeze."

Conner rolled his eyes. "You're paranoid." He started for the family room.

I went to the kitchen, ready to drown spiders in spray. But there weren't any. I squirted the corners for good measure, then stuffed the Raid in my pocket. I moved slow so it wouldn't come out. I passed the main house and kept going.

A leaf landed on my head. Others dropped to the ground. I watched them fall, glad I wasn't one of them. A branch shook above me, sending more leaves to the earth.

"Conner, did you see that?"

"See what?"

"Up there." I pointed to the top of the tree. "A branch shook."

"No, it didn't," he said.

There was no point in arguing. I decided to scrap our plan. "Wait up!" I caught up with him near the family room.

Conner gave me a look, but let me stay. He eased into the family room and opened fire. I waited below. I held my spray can, ready. I had yet to see any spiders, but it sounded like Conner had stumbled on the mother lode. At his command, I joined him. I expected to find spider legs and eyes soaked and dying. But I didn't.

Flies and mosquitoes floated in the clear poison. That's it.

"Where are the spiders?" I asked.

"You got me." Conner poked his head out of the window, then brought it back inside. A day ago he would have had a hefty red spider in his blond hair. Not now.

Not finding any spiders was almost worse than finding them. I did a slow three-sixty. I studied the darkness. Nothing but twigs and leaves. The spiders had to be out there. Beyond the stream of our triggers. Watching. Planning.

"Ouch!" Something bit me. I slapped my neck and checked my hand. A squashed mosquito stuck to my palm.

We edged to the open section of the family room and scanned the tree. The webs were gone. No funnels. No wheels of white silk. No strands of web dangling from twigs. Nothing.

"Looks like someone beat us to the punch," Conner said.

"Maybe Mr. Scopula came and wiped them all out. Maybe he really believed the Giant Orb Weaver was deadly."

Conner didn't buy it. "How could *all* the spiders be gone?" He slapped at the mosquito on his leg and sprayed at insects flying nearby.

One landed on my arm a second later. I killed it just as a horsefly bit my shin. We slapped and sprayed the insects that clouded around us. With no spiders in the tree, the other bugs were having a field day. I wanted to leave, but Conner decided that we should spray as much of the tree as possible. The insects would die sooner or later and the spiders wouldn't come back.

We climbed from room to room. We soaked the wood with poison, then moved on. We traversed the rope bridge enroute to a platform. Halfway out, we paused. Something black leapt through the branches near the top of the tree. The darkness and dense leaves did their job. We couldn't see what it was or where it went. Conner picked up the pace. "Come on, Sis."

I could tell he was scared.

I scrambled along the rope bridge, trying to hurry. Conner was a ways in front. I tripped and went down. The can of Raid dropped from my hand and fell to the ground. It landed on a rock and exploded. Branches shook in the tree top. The animal crawled through the outer leaves. I couldn't identify it. Just a fuzzy image. Black. Or brown. About three feet long, or four. Six legs, maybe more. A white line trailed behind it.

"Jaime, get up!" Conner shouted.

I pulled myself to my feet. But one foot was stuck between a branch and the rope. The creature descended, still hidden in darkness and leaves. It moved in for the kill. Branches shifted. Leaves fell. I jerked my foot until my shoe came off. I didn't care. I was free. More movement behind me. Closer. I glanced over my shoulder. I caught a glimpse of the legs. The fuzzy body and head. Then it disappeared.

I screamed and rushed across the rope bridge to Conner. He pulled me onto the platform, then stepped between me and the creature.

"What do you think it is?" I asked.

"I don't know."

"You're not going to fight it with that, are you?" I patted the gallon of pesticide on his back.

Conner looked at the spray nozzle with disdain, like it was a pea shooter and he was hunting a bear. "Climb down, Jaime. Hurry!"

I backed down the wood boards nailed to the limb. Conner followed. We kept on guard every step of the way. The creature descended as we did, keeping out of sight. More strands of white silk appeared. They looked as thick as nylon rope, and just as strong. We reached the main house and rushed inside. It was dark. Spooky. We couldn't hear the creature. Or see it. I swallowed and held my breath.

A twig creaked just outside the window. I snapped my head around and stared at it. I wasn't about to poke my head out there. Neither was Conner.

Then something hit the roof. We stared at the ceiling for what might come through. It was up there. Conner held both hands on the pistol sprayer, ready to fire.

"Go down, Jaime. We're almost there."

"I can't. What if it's out there?" I sat in the corner of the main house.

Conner glanced down the hatch. "I'll go first. But you stay right behind me."

"Don't worry," I told him. I edged to the hatch as Conner lowered through it. Suddenly having him go first didn't seem like such a great idea. I was alone in the tree house in the dark. The window didn't have drapes or glass. If something wanted to rush in, it could. The open end that led to the view deck wasn't far away.

The roof creaked. Something moved across it. "Hurry, Conner," I whimpered.

He told me it was hard to see the wood rungs in the dark. I sat on the edge of the hatch with my feet dangling through it. I watched the window. And the deck. The roof moaned. The animal headed for the open end. It was out of sight, but there.

"Hurry, Conner!" I stepped on the first rung. But I was still in the house from the waist up.

At first I thought it was a branch. It curled under the ceiling. It was black and sharp. Over two feet long. Not a paw or an arm. It was the leg of a spider.

Chapter 13

My parents didn't believe us. We stood in the kitchen gasping for breath. I pushed against my ribs to ease my side ache.

"It was giant," Conner gasped. "Four feet across. Easy."

"Easy," I repeated. I went to the refrigerator for a glass of water.

My dad watched me gulp it down. "A four-foot spider?" He looked at my mom for her reaction. She raised her eyebrows and shrugged.

Conner described what had happened from the time we arrived at the tree house until we ran home. He pointed to my shoeless foot as proof. "I think we should call animal control. Or maybe the game warden."

My mom eyed my filthy sock. I could tell she wasn't happy. "You ran home without your shoe?"

"And my tools?" Dad added.

"We had to." I filled the glass again.

"I'm still having trouble with a four-foot spider," my dad said. He held up his hands to show us what a four-foot spider would look like.

Conner got defensive. "Jaime said it was a spider, not me. I just know *something* was there."

I didn't like how quickly he backed down.

My dad closed his hands by a foot. "How about a three foot opossum? They're climbers."

I stomped to the window and glared out at the night. "Dad, I think I know the difference between an opossum and a spider."

"What about a raccoon?" Mom suggested. "Or a vulture?"

Conner bit his lip and made eye contact with me, as if to say, *What did you expect?* At first, it made me mad. But I couldn't blame him, or my parents. My story was definitely a stretch. A four-foot spider was unheard of. Impossible. But I couldn't deny what I'd seen.

My dad tried changing the subject. "Listen, since you two are into fixing things up, how about helping me around here? I found a porch swing in the basement that needs some work."

I didn't answer. Neither did Conner. The sound of drops on the back porch told us it was starting to rain.

"I think they're still in the magnolia tree," my mom said to my dad.

"I guess so," he admitted. He paused at the screen door to grab an umbrella. "I don't think animal control or the game warden will take you seriously, not from what you told us. You need more evidence. Take a picture next time. Or better yet, trap the thing."

Conner shrugged. "We could do that."

"How?" I asked.

"That's what I'd like to know," my mom added. She crossed her arms and used her eyebrows to rebuke my dad. She obviously wasn't happy about us returning to the tree.

"Get a book on traps," Dad said. "You can—"

"Don't say it," Conner interrupted. He covered his ears.

"—go to the library." My dad grinned. "It's only a short bike ride away."

Mom liked that idea. "The rain should be gone by tomorrow."

"Along with the poison we sprayed in the mag tree," Conner mumbled. He complained for what seemed like forever, but finally gave in. "As long as we're back by the afternoon to set the trap."

That was fine with me. I just wanted a few minutes with the librarian. She needed to know Mr. Scopula wasn't an expert after all.

I also wanted to see whether the spider books had been returned. In the meantime, I decided to check my field guide to read up on the world's largest spiders. It's not that I thought I'd find a four footer, but I figured the more I learned about spiders, the better. I changed into my PJs, stretched out on my bed, and opened the book. The close-up color pictures were amazing—too real, like the spiders could crawl right off the pages. The Mexican Red-Knee Tarantula had furry legs like pipe cleaners. The Giant Orb Weaver's legs were bony and stretched seven inches across. Its body was shiny like chrome.

One diagram offered a cross section of a spider's body. The rear half, that looked like its bottom, was actually called its abdomen. That's where the heart was. For some reason I never thought spiders had one. The silk glands were at the rear of the abdomen. Spiders made webs by pulling the silk out with their legs. The pictures of webs reminded me of the ones in the giant tree. Sheets of white, some haphazard, some in perfect symmetry. Funnels. Hammocks. Scribbles of white silk in the air. They were amazing.

The Crab Spider was as yellow as a daisy. The Triangle Spider looked like a piece of Indian jewelry, with intricate orange patterns. The Ladybug Spider looked just like it sounds, with a red abdomen and black dots. I turned another page, amazed that I hadn't mumbled "gross" once.

Then I got to the section on fangs. Spiders have two of them, which point together like pinchers. The book described them as hollow needles that venom flows through. A picture showed a Rusty Wandering Spider sinking its fangs into a tree frog. Another photo had a tarantula's fangs piercing the skin of a baby mouse. That did it for me. "Ga-ross!"

"I heard that," Conner shouted from down the hall.

I closed the book and fished a quarter from my purse. That time it was worth it. I'd seen enough. The clock next to my bed said 11:30 P.M. I couldn't believe I had read for so long. I turned off the light. I stared at the darkness and let my eyes adjust. The cardboard and duct tape on my window had partially come loose.

The old house smelled its age. The air felt damp from the rain. Muggy. I didn't need my sheet, but I wanted it for protection. I brought it to my chin and clutched it. Not that a sheet could stop a four-foot spider. But maybe it would ward off the ones I had just read about, the tarantulas and black widows.

Moon shadows danced on my wall. The twigs resembled claws and spiders on the move. I watched the cracks in the baseboard, wondering how many spiders lived there and why we had to buy such an old house.

I closed my eyes and prayed, convinced sleep would be impossible. I said my verse over and over. "If God is for us, who can be against us."

That must have done the trick. The next thing I knew, it was the middle of the night and I was waking up to go to the bathroom. My book was on the floor and opened to a blank page. That seemed weird, but I kept going. The hardwood floor creaked beneath my feet. The bathroom door squeaked when I closed it behind me.

At the same time, the nightlight shut off. I gave it a whack. It came back on. But one look, and I wished it was off again. A tarantula crawled across the mirror at eye level. It was the size of a man's hand, with fangs ready to attack.

I screamed and stepped back. A Giant Orb Weaver dropped from the ceiling just inches from my face. I swatted it away, but it clung to my hand. I shook violently until it came off, but that didn't help. Spiders streamed from the vent in the ceiling. They dropped in my hair and on my arms. I tried to scream, but couldn't. My voice was gone.

I twisted and flung my arms wildly. I jumped and kicked. I stomped the spiders to a pulp. But more crawled from under the baseboards. All varieties. Widows. Orbs. Tarantulas. Jumping Spiders. Wolf Spiders. I grabbed the doorknob. Locked. I twisted with all my strength. Locked.

I screamed with a raspy voice. Spiders climbed my legs. Dropped on my neck. I pounded the door. Still locked. No one came. I went for the shower. My last hope. I could wash them off. Spiders covered the white porcelain. Black ones. Brown ones. Red. Yellow. I jumped in with my bare feet. They crawled over my toes. Up my shins. I turned on the hot water full blast.

No water.

Spiders poured from the shower head. They buried my face and hair.

I let out a bloodcurdling scream. More spiders converged. From the drain. The toilet. Electrical outlets. My parents didn't come. Neither did Conner. They were already gone. Wrapped in webs and eaten alive.

I stepped from the tub. The medicine cabinet flew open. A spider's leg followed. Black and shiny. Two feet long. Deadly. Another leg. Eight eyes. Fangs like meat hooks. The giant tree spider had followed me home.

It dropped to the counter and shot me with silk. The web hit my chest. My hands. I fought back. I tore at the silk. I yanked it away and threw it down. But it kept coming. Around my arms. My stomach. My throat. I couldn't breathe. I couldn't stand. I fell to the ground. I twisted and fought. I had to get free. But I couldn't. The spider balanced on the edge of the counter. Our eyes met for a horrible moment.

Then it flashed its fangs and jumped.

Chapter 14

The spider landed on my shoulder. I rolled to my stomach, kicking and screaming. The web tightened around my throat. I yanked at the white silk strangling me.

Then a voice reached me. It was Conner. "Jaime!"

"Get it off!" I wailed.

"Wake up!" He shook me. "Jaime, wake up!"

I opened my eyes. Daylight streamed past the cardboard and duct tape. My white sheet had come untucked and wrapped around my throat.

Conner sat on the edge of my bed, watching me. "Good morning, psycho. Pleasant dreams?"

I unwrapped the sheet from my neck. I took a moment to get my bearings. "That was the worst nightmare of my life."

"At least you didn't say gross." Conner stood and started for the door. "Now get up. Let's get this library thing over with."

The clock said 10:00 A.M. I had overslept. I got dressed and met Conner at the kitchen table. Over a bowl of cereal he told me that Mom had gone shopping and Dad had left for work. He had spent the last hour practicing with his bow and arrow, just in case the trap didn't work. It was obvious he didn't want it to, not if he could kill the animal instead. He was so excited about his progress, he had me come outside to watch him. I stood behind him with my bowl of cereal.

He pulled the arrow to his cheek and let go. It shot straight for the cardboard. Too bad it was the cardboard in my window.

"Nice one," I said. "Good thing I'm down here."

Conner stared at his bow as if someone had tampered with it. He grabbed another arrow and let it fly. It didn't just hit the box. It hit the bull's-eye.

"Not bad," I said. "I could have used you in my nightmare." As I filled him in, I found myself reliving it. I tried to put the spiders out of my mind, but couldn't. The images were too vivid. Too real. I hoped it was nothing more than the consequence of reading the book late at night. But something told me that it was more than that.

Something deeper . . . and deadly. I had a feeling that we were close to solving it. But instead of making me happy, I had a feeling that the worst was yet come.

The ride to the library didn't take long. I practiced how I would tell the librarian that her expert didn't know what he was talking about. She had seemed to think the world of the guy.

"Just tell her the truth," Conner told me. He had me bring along Mr. Scopula's note and the field guide to show the contradiction.

I found the librarian at the information counter running the scanner over books. She let us stand there for a minute before acknowledging us. "Can I help you?"

I unfolded the note and showed her what Mr. Scopula had written. "Is there any way I could meet him? I need to talk with him about this note."

"You do, huh?"

"Yeah. Not to be mean or anything, but it's not right." I opened the field guide to the page with the Giant Orb Weaver. "This is what I described, and it doesn't say anything about them being deadly."

The librarian didn't even look at the photo. "Could it be that the spider he listed comes in other varieties that fit the description you gave him?"

"The book doesn't say anything about other varieties that are poisonous to humans."

"Maybe you should check another book," she suggested.

"Were the others returned?"

She checked her computer. "I'm afraid not."

I could tell that Conner was getting antsy. I let out a breath of frustration. "Is there some way we could talk to Mr. Scopula? There are other spiders I'd like to ask him about. One in particular. It was big."

The librarian eyed me doubtfully. "I can ask him to contact you, but . . ." she let her sentence trail off, her eyes fixed on someone over my shoulder. I spun around and caught a glimpse of a face before it ducked behind a book shelf. I recognized the hair and fair skin.

It was Dean Hilton.

My chin dropped. I sputtered his name. "D-d-de—"

"What's wrong?" Conner asked.

"D-dean," I pointed. "That was Dean Hilton."

"You're sure?"

"It was him," I insisted. I described what he looked like and took off in pursuit. I rushed through the reading tables and desks. Conner followed. When I got to the row where he had been, it was empty. I pointed for Conner to take one direction. I took another.

Dean's mop of black hair rounded a corner in front of me. I followed. His sleeve disappeared down a row as I arrived. "Conner, over here." I sent him ahead for the cutoff.

I rushed down an aisle. I jogged, then ran.

Bits of Dean Hilton appeared, then disappeared. His black hair. A shoulder. A hand. His dark eyes between the books. Conner worked one side of the room, I worked the other. We kept Dean in front of us, moving him toward the end of the long room.

We checked everything we came to, reading cubicles, computer workstations, magazine racks. We couldn't find him. Once, we thought we had him, but he mysteriously got away. We moved down the aisles, checking row after row of books. Conner and I made eye contact before the last row. We nodded, knowing Dean had run out of options. I counted with my fingers. One. Two. Three.

We swept around the end.

A kid buried his face in a book.

"Gotcha," Conner said.

The kid dropped the book, stunned. He had dark hair, but he wasn't Dean.

"We're looking for Dean Hilton. Have you seen him?" I asked.

"Dean Hilton?" he repeated, acting surprised. "N-no." He watched us with big eyes, then hurried away. He kept checking back as he rounded the shelves.

I stood with Conner in the otherwise empty row. I wondered if the kid had told the truth. "Something's not right. I know I saw him. Where could he have gone?"

"I think I know." Conner pointed to a door marked Employees Only.

"You think?" I asked.

Conner nodded. "Go for it."

I hesitated, but not for long. I knocked on the door. No response. I turned the brass knob. Unlocked.

"Hello?" I offered, knocking again. Nothing. I opened the door and stepped quickly into a large office. Conner followed. We closed the door behind us. A long walnut desk had a matching executive chair behind it. A sectional couch filled the corner. We searched under the desk and behind the door. Conner looked in a closet.

No Dean Hilton.

We turned to leave, but never made it.

The door swung open.

"What are you doing in here?" an angry voice asked.

Chapter 15

The librarian glared at us until I thought her eyes—magnified by her glasses—were going to pop.

"Um . . ." I started off. "We're looking for someone."

"Not in here, you're not." She pointed to the sign on the door.

"I know . . . it's just that . . . we were . . . ." I cut myself off. There was nothing to hide. I spilled the beans. I told the librarian about the memorial cross and Dean Hilton's name carved in the wood. Conner filled in what I left out. The only thing we skipped was the animal that nearly ate us for a bedtime snack.

The librarian walked behind the desk. "Hmm. The magnolia tree strikes again."

"You know about it?" I asked.

"Unfortunately, yes. Take Mr. Scopula's advice. Stay away." She wrote something out on a piece of paper and folded it in half. I thought she would give it to me, but she didn't. Instead, she ushered us from the office. "Dean Hilton wasn't here today."

"But I saw—"

"That wasn't him. You confused him with someone else." She put the piece of paper in my hand and closed my fingers around it. She turned to leave, then stopped. "You can find Dean at that address."

I unfolded the paper. Conner read over my shoulder. We were new in town, so the street and number meant nothing to us—at least not yet.

"Are you ready?" I asked.

Conner pulled my wrist. "Let's go."

We rode through town. We passed brick buildings that looked as old as the nation. Some brown. Others red. White columns fronted the courthouse. An American flag waved above the police station. The sign on the Stockgrower's State Bank gave the current time and temperature. Eleven-thirty A.M. Ninety-two degrees. I asked Conner if he wanted to stop for a drink. He didn't, so we kept riding. The anticipation of meeting Dean Hilton drove us. Forget about thirst. Forget about rest. We had too many unanswered questions. Why was there a cross under the tree with his name on it? Had he started to build the treehouse? If so, why didn't he finish it? Did he know about the spiders and the giant creature that looked like one?

"Can't be much further," Conner wheezed.

The businesses gave way to parks and schools. We passed our new church and kept riding.

"That should be it," I said. I pointed to a two-story white house up ahead. It reminded me of a colonial estate. The mowed and trimmed lawns around it belonged on a golf course.

"That's some house," Conner said.

We turned into the circular drive. What we couldn't see from down the street, we could see now. We weren't at a house or someone's private estate. The gold plaque next to the door read Merrifield Memorial Gardens.

"Is this what I think it is?" I ventured.

Conner put his feet down to balance himself. "Looks like you were right about Dean Hilton."

"Maybe he works here," I suggested.

"I doubt it."

We parked our bikes and headed inside. The man at the reception desk looked up Dean's name, then wrote out a row and plot number for us to check. We walked the path reading headstones until we came to Dean's. We were right about the cross. The years for his birth and death matched. The inscription quoted the Twenty-third Psalm: *The Lord is my Shepherd, I shall not be in want. He makes me lie down in green pastures.*

Conner walked around the grave, then met me at the headstone. His reaction surprised me. "Fifteen. Same age as me."

"No wonder the librarian wanted us to avoid the tree," I said. "Mr. Scopula must have told her what was there."

"He should have told Dean."

"Maybe he did."

"He didn't tell us."

"He warned us to stay away. If he'd said there was a deadly creature in that tree, would you have believed him?"

Conner didn't answer. He looked at the grave and bounced on his feet. Something was boiling inside him.

"What's wrong?" I asked.

Without a word, Conner hurried along the path toward the giant house. "See you at home," he called back over his shoulder.

"Wait up," I said. I followed him inside.

"Did you find him?" the mortician asked.

I nodded and kept going, trying to keep up with Conner. By the time I got outside, he had climbed on his bike and had taken off.

"What's wrong?" I yelled, getting on my bike.

"Don't worry about it."

"Conner!" I shouted.

He stood up and peddled. "I need to get ready."

"Ready for what?" I gasped.

"You know."

"Don't tell me you're going back there?"

He didn't. But he didn't need to. He rode with conviction. Fury. I tried to keep up, but couldn't. I called after him, but he wouldn't slow down. Soon he disappeared around a corner. Out of sight. I prayed that God would protect him. That I'd see him alive again.

But my mind turned dark. Terrible. I pictured the giant spider waiting in its web, ready to pounce. I feared that if Conner didn't calm down, Dean Hilton wouldn't be the last fifteen-year-old with his name on a cross beneath the tree.

Chapter 16

When I reached our house, I dropped my bike in the front yard and ran inside. "Conner!"

No answer.

"Mom!" I shouted. "Don't let Conner go to the tree house."

I couldn't see her, but figured she was in the laundry room or family room or kitchen. She would hear me.

She wasn't. And didn't.

I jogged upstairs to my parent's bedroom. Then to Conner's. I went back downstairs. To the den. I shouted into the basement. No answer. Our house was deserted.

I checked the back yard as a last resort. There I saw Conner gripping his bow and pulling the string to his cheek.

"Finally!" I blurted out.

He released the arrow. It sailed over the box into the field. "That's your fault," he told me.

I didn't argue. If he spent the day searching for the arrow instead of returning to the spider tree, that would be fine with me.

"Where's Mom?" I asked him.

Conner pulled another arrow from his quiver. "Gone. She left a message on the machine."

I went back inside and listened to it. My mom explained that after she finished her errands, she would meet my dad at work. They had to fill out some forms regarding the sale of our house. Afterward, they were meeting my dad's new boss for dinner. They'd be home late. Leftovers were in the fridge.

I went to the window and watched Conner fire another arrow. It sailed wide, landing in the grass. I knew what he was thinking. But he couldn't hit a box the size of a phone booth. How could he hit a mysterious creature crawling through a tree? Without my mom to stop him, it was up to me.

I pushed through the door and marched to Conner's side. "You can't go through with this."

"Yes I can."

"Why? To get a cross with your name on it?" I yanked his arm. "You want to be like Dean Hilton?"

"Won't happen." Conner jerked free a
a quick shot. It hit the box.

"You heard what the librarian said. What Mr. Scopula said. Stay away."

Conner released another arrow. It landed in front of the box. "So we stay away, then what? What happens when other kids climb the tree? When they get killed, what's everyone going to say?"

I didn't bother to answer. I had heard this before.

"They're going to say, 'Someone must have known about that thing. Why didn't they do something about it?' Then how will you feel?"

"I'm not saying we shouldn't do anything. But why should we be the ones to kill it?"

"Sure. Let someone else do it. What a cop-out."

"It's not a cop-out. There are experts for this sort of thing. Like animal control. Or the—"

Conner cut me off. "You heard Dad. They'd laugh at us." Conner yanked the bow string and shot an arrow. It hit the box. It even hit the target. "You can stay back if you want. But I'm going to the tree."

I left for my bedroom in a huff. I opened my Bible to Romans 8 and read the whole chapter. I said my favorite verse out loud when I came to it. "If God is for us, who can be against us?" I

ased on how I felt. "How
d a million of its friends."
I said that. I didn't want to
could do. But I couldn't help

open on my lap, I prayed for a
lon nner and the Hilton family. I also
prayed fo t might happen in the magnolia
tree.

Tidying up my room came next. I hoped it would calm me down. I put away the laundry my mom had stacked on my dresser. I unrolled a poster and hung it from the wall. When a fly buzzed, I found the swatter and flattened it with one swing. I gave it another swat for good measure.

I held the swatter and surveyed my room. A spider crawled from a crack in the baseboard. Bad timing. I had too much pent up anger. I went after it with a vengeance. I whacked the floor, but missed. I swung again. It dodged me and ran under the chair. I tossed the chair aside. The spider scurried across the floor for my bed. *Whack! Whack!* Two more misses.

I rolled my bed aside but couldn't find the spider. "Come out, you chicken." I sat down on my bed and started to cry. I hated our house. The cracks and creaks. The spiders and bugs. Classic, nothing. It was a dump. An ugly old dump.

"Gross!" I shouted. "Gross! Gross! Gross!"

I went to my purse and removed a dollar. I took it to the kitchen and slapped it on the counter. Why'd we have to move? I thought of my parents signing the final papers today. What if something went wrong? Maybe the buyers would change their minds. We could move back to our other house. To the nice carpet. New fixtures. Clean walls with perfect joints. No cracks. No gaps. No spiders.

I went to the bathroom for a tissue, then checked on Conner. He was firing shot after shot. Some hit the bull's-eye. Others flew wide. I figured he'd call it quits anytime, but he didn't. He spent the rest of the day practicing. He took a break for dinner, but that's about it. I tried to discourage him from going back to the tree, but I couldn't.

At seven, he took his arrows to the garage to sharpen the arrowheads. Then he came inside and packed his stuff like a soldier prepares for war. I did the same—under protest.

I put on a long sleeve shirt and jeans to protect me from the spiders. Clouds had moved in, which gave some relief from the heat, but not enough. Sweat darkened my shirt in patches.

Conner fastened a looped rope to his waist. He put his quiver over his shoulder. He slipped a pocket knife in his jeans.

I stuffed a fanny pack with bandages. Antiseptic. Medical tape. Aspirin. Tweezers. Conner added a flashlight and canteen.

"No weapons?" Conner asked.

I shook my head.

He went to his room and came back with a throwing knife. "Just in case."

I put it in my fanny pack and zipped it up.

"Ready?" Conner asked.

"No."

"Great. Let's do it. For Dean Hilton."

He marched to the porch. I followed. We paused there to look at the tree. I racked my brain for a way to stall or get Conner to call it off. I said stuff about waiting for Dad's approval, calling for help. Anything. But Conner wouldn't listen. His mind was made up. He jumped from the porch to the yard.

Then the phone rang.

I ran inside and answered it. A muffled voice said, "This is Mr. Scopula."

Chapter 17

"Is this Jaime?" he asked softly.

I told him that it was and asked why he described the Giant Orb spider as deadly.

"I wanted you to be careful, to stay away from the tree," Mr. Scopula said. The deep pitch in his voice didn't sound right, like it was forced.

"Then you know about the giant spider?" I went on.

"Yes." He told me he had been to the tree. He'd seen the giant spider and the hundreds of others. "Take my advice, Jaime. Don't go back."

"Tell my brother that," I said.

"Put him on."

I put my hand over the phone. "Conner, he wants to talk to you."

"I'm leaving."

I raised my voice. "Conner!"

He glared at me while grabbing the receiver. I almost went for the other phone, but decided to stay put.

Conner rolled his eyes at me while listening to Mr. Scopula. "I know. We saw his memorial." He made a hurry-up motion with his hand. "It's all right. We'll be careful."

Mr. Scopula said something else, then Conner hung up.

"Well, what'd he say?" I asked.

"Nothing new. The tree's dangerous. Stay away."

"Did he tell you how Dean Hilton died?"

"Not specifically. In the tree, somehow." Conner walked to the back porch. "Are you coming or not?"

I stood there, baffled. "You're still going?"

"With or without you," Conner told me. "That Scopula guy has already proven we can't trust him. And what's with his voice?"

"Who cares?" I said. "He just wanted to keep us away from the spider tree. And now we know why."

"We don't know anything," Conner said. "Not really." He started across the back yard without another word. I trailed behind, but at a distance. I didn't want to go. But even more than that, I didn't want my brother to go alone.

Before climbing the magnolia tree, we stepped through the tall weeds to the cross with Dean's name on it. It was Conner's idea. He closed his eyes and told me to do the same. He said a prayer for Dean's family. He also prayed for God to help him kill whatever had killed Dean.

Even after Conner said amen, I didn't want to look up. I kept thinking of the time when a thousand spiders had rained down. That didn't stop Conner. He searched the limbs and leaves while moving toward the massive trunk. He noticed me stalling at the cross. "What are you waiting for?"

I took my time getting to him and stood moping on the raised roots.

Conner checked his equipment, slung his bow over his shoulder, then started to climb. Moments later, he disappeared inside the main house.

"Well?" I called up.

He poked his head from the window and held his finger against his lips to shush me. I made a "what?" gesture with my hands. He waved me up without a sound. I tightened my fanny pack and started to climb. I tentatively poked my head through the floor hatch. Conner squatted in the corner. He held his bow, already loaded with an arrow. After a quick check for spiders, I climbed all the way in.

"See anything?" I whispered.

Conner shook his head. "We'll wait."

We did.

Conner kept his bow in hand, ready to shoot. After what seemed like an hour, he waddled to the view deck. He scanned the upper branches, then returned. He motioned for me to poke my head through the window and have a look.

I shook my head. That didn't go over well.

Conner's eyebrows came together in an angry bar. I tightened my lips and looked at the window. I didn't want to go there. The silence was unreal, like the entire grove was holding its breath. I know I was.

In the span of a heartbeat, I stuck my head through the window, checked the walls and branches, then brought it back inside. "Nothing," I whispered.

Conner wasn't convinced. He edged me aside to look for himself. I crawled for a corner but never made it. Something stung my hand. I hit the ceiling. "Yeouch!"

"What?" Conner blurted out. He drew his bow, ready to shoot.

"Ouch!" I grabbed my wrist and shook it. "Something bit me!"

Conner aimed at the floor. "Where? Where? I don't see it! What was it?"

"I don't know." I calmed down enough to look at the sting. A sliver of wood protruded from my palm. A drop of blood trickled from the puncture and slid down my wrist.

"That's just a splinter," Conner complained. He slowly released his bow.

I could tell he was mad at me, like I had done something wrong. I wasn't about to argue. A splinter was fine with me. I opened my first aid kit and got out the tweezers. I removed the splinter, then applied antiseptic. I concluded with a bandage. Conner watched me play nurse while making occasional trips to the view deck.

"Anything?" I whispered. I put everything away and zipped up my fanny pouch.

"We're too early. But that's OK. I'd rather ambush *it,* than vice-versa." He motioned for me to join him on the view deck. When I got there, he cupped his hand over my ear. "I know where it lives."

"You do?"

Conner pointed at the widow's watch near the top of the tree. "It probably sleeps there during the day, then comes out at night. But don't worry," he told me. "I've got a plan."

I followed Conner to the family room.

"You watch the widow's watch from here. I'll watch it from the crow's nest." He unzipped my fanny pouch and put the throwing knife in my hand. He put the flashlight in his pocket.

"What's this for?" I moaned. The knife felt cool in my hand—and awkward.

"In case it gets by me . . . you know." Conner tightened his lips. I could tell he was scared, but he forced a smile. He told me to be patient and tough, then made his way to the crow's nest.

I hunkered down in the family room. The plywood felt rough against my back. I stretched my legs and tried to get comfortable. My face burned. I could tell it was red. My long sleeve shirt and pants didn't help. The still air offered no relief. My hands sparkled with sweat. I wiped my forehead, but that only transferred sweat from one part of my body to another. I pushed the point of the throwing knife into my wrist and grimaced. Conner had sharpened the blade along with the arrowheads.

I studied the widow's watch for signs of the dark creature. Nothing. I checked my watch. Eight o'clock. Conner arrived in the crow's nest. He made some noise loading an arrow onto his bow, but was silent after that. Ten minutes passed. Eight-ten. Still nothing.

I established a visual surveillance route to keep busy. Stay alert. I began with the outer branches that touched an oak tree. The widow's watch came next, followed by Conner. Then the kitchen. The main house. The ground. I paused for a ten count at each location. When I finished, I started over. The routine was mesmerizing. My adrenaline began to subside, then drain altogether. Too many sleepless nights caught up with me. I fought to stay awake. But my eyelids wouldn't cooperate. They had their own agenda. I allowed them a few seconds of rest. They wanted more. I conceded to a minute—max. That turned into five. They still weren't satisfied.

The next thing I knew, Conner was nudging me with a stick.

I opened my eyes.

It wasn't Conner. It wasn't a stick.

A pointed black leg reached through the window and caught me.

Chapter 18

I screamed and clove into the corner. The leg withdrew. I caught a glimpse of an eye beneath shiny black hair.

"Get away from her!" Conner shouted.

The giant spider jumped from the family room and swung on a strand of web. An arrow sliced through the branches. It just missed.

"Conner!" I screamed.

He stood on the crow's nest, loading another arrow. The creature landed on a limb, paused, then returned. Conner pulled his bowstring to his cheek and released an arrow. It nicked the white line. The spider creature swung toward me. I fumbled for the knife, but dropped it. The spider kept coming. "Conner!" I wailed.

He let out a war cry.

I got hold of the knife and squeezed the handle. The animal closed in. The dark legs. Multiple eyes.

Hairy face. Spider. Human. Neither. Both. I held the blade in front of me with both hands, trembling. Closer. Ten feet. Five.

The spider dropped out of sight.

"Conner, where is it?" I got to my knees. I still couldn't see it. I climbed to my feet and stood in the center of the family room. "Conner?"

"I can't find it," he shouted, his voice frantic.

I turned in circles. I clutched the knife with both hands. I didn't blink. I watched everything. The walls. The window. The branches. Something moved. I shrieked.

Conner dug the flashlight from his pocket. He shined it all around. He moved the beam over limbs and leaves. He checked the widow's watch. The kitchen and main house. Nothing.

"Let's get out of here," I said. But even as I said it, I knew we couldn't leave. There was no way out above, and with the spider below, I wasn't going down.

"There it is!" Conner shouted. He put down the flashlight and loaded his bow. He shot an arrow toward the main house. THUMP! The arrowhead embedded in the plywood siding. The creature disappeared in the gray light.

Conner tossed me his flashlight. I made the catch and pointed the beam at the main house. The giant spider scrambled up a limb. It moved like it was injured. Only four of the legs seemed to be working. Something wasn't right. The spider scurried along the backside, keeping out of sight. I tried to follow it with the flashlight. I caught glimpses of its feet. It kept climbing, higher than me, but on the opposite side of the tree. It passed Conner.

"What's it doing?" I asked, hysterical.

"I know," Conner said. "And I'm ready." He drew his bow to his cheek.

The giant spider swung from behind the limb. Its body was brown with black legs. I kept the light on target.

Conner shot again. Way off. The spider pounced. It landed on the limb above Conner. The one that led to the widow's watch. It climbed with speed and ease. It kept the tree between itself and Conner. Conner moved around the crow's nest to get a clear shot.

The spider moved too. I kept the light on it. For a second the beam caught its head. It had multiple dark eyes—some not real. Fuzzy hair covered the face, then lifted. I caught a glimpse of pale skin. Teeth, not fangs. A nose. I saw more. Just fragments. The short leg. Deformed. It didn't make sense. Not spider. Not human.

"Almost got it," Conner shouted.

"Wait," I said. "Wait a second!" The face came to me. I'd seen it.

It let out a cry and hurried for the widow's watch.

But Conner was raging. He leaned way out to get a shot.

"NO!" I screamed.

Conner stretched. Too far.

The crow's nest cracked.

Conner grabbed at the limb. His arms flailed. But he couldn't stop himself. For a second he seemed suspended in air. Then he plunged.

"Conner!" I wailed. I scrambled from the family room. Through the main house and around the spiral trunk ladder. I rushed through the tall grass to my brother. He didn't move.

A sound came from the tree top. A piercing cry. Sorrow. Anguish.

I held Conner's hand and put my head against his chest. His heart was beating. For now.

Branches snapped above me. Leaves shook. It swung from web to limb to web. The sounds trailed away. From tree to tree.

Then it vanished.

I held Conner's hand until sirens filled the night. Until my parents came running across the field shouting our names. Until the paramedics in the red truck bounced to the base of the magnolia tree.

But I kept seeing that face. The fair skin and deep-set eyes.

And I knew.

Chapter 19

It was a week before I returned to the magnolia tree. Conner had a broken leg and two cracked ribs. Fortunately he hadn't landed on his head. I busied myself with taking care of him or helping Dad with the house. We finished the porch swing and brought it up from the basement. Every day I'd swing on it and wait for the mail. I'd rush to the curb, hoping to find a letter from Sarah or Katy.

My dad thought it strange that I would ever go back to the tree. But I had to. I had to know for sure.

The paramedic who helped Conner had come two years earlier when Dean Hilton fell to his death. I learned that in both cases the call for help came from the same person. When the paramedic told me who, it all made sense.

But that wasn't enough. I had to meet him. I had to hear his side of it so I could understand and forgive.

I climbed the spiral rungs that wound around the massive trunk. The spiders were back in full force. They scurried away, not wanting any part of me. The feeling was mutual.

A Giant Orb Weaver was waiting for me in the main house. Its seven foot web stretched from floor to ceiling, from wall to wall. Its long orange and black legs clung to the center of the web. I couldn't slip by it, so I climbed out the window and onto the roof. From there I crossed to the limb that led to the family room. A messy tangle of white silk stretched across the window. A funnel web filled a corner. I stood in the center of the room with my arms wrapped around me. I didn't know what to say, or how to say it, so I just started with his name.

"Daren?" I called out. I watched the widow's watch for his face to appear over the side. "Daren? It's me, Jaime. Conner's sister."

His mop of black hair appeared. His face came next. His eyes watched me from deep in their dark sockets. I waited for him to say something, but he didn't. I stared at his round face, chalky, timid. I remembered seeing him in the library. His was the deformed hand holding the newspaper, the one that made me think of the G word. He was the one we chased toward the employee office.

He was Dean's little brother.

"I want to talk to you," I told him.

He disappeared in the widow's watch. A minute later his deformed hand appeared. He waved me up. His words were simple and haunting. "Come here."

A fuzzy brown spider stood guard between me and the limb that led there. "Um . . ."

Somehow Daren knew about the spider. "He won't hurt you. Just let him be."

I swallowed and started up. The spider moved out of sight. I kept thinking it would reappear and sink its fangs into my fingers. But I didn't rush or lose my cool. I couldn't—not after what happened to Conner.

When I made it to the cracked crow's nest, I decided I had climbed high enough. I clung to the limb and whispered my verse. My heart thumped against the bark.

"Higher," Daren said. He motioned for me to keep coming, to join him in the widow's watch. I told him I was fine where I was.

He peered over the side. "I'm sorry about your brother. I never meant to hurt him."

"Then why'd you do all that stuff?" I asked. I knew he was the one who had haunted us. Here.

At home. In the library. I drew my knees to my chin. I watched more and more spiders appear. They crept from cracks in the bark. From the plastic green leaves. They converged like an army toward Daren . . . and me.

"You would have killed them all . . . sooner or later. You're like I used to be. Before Dean . . ." Daren's words trailed off. His eyes fell.

I didn't know how to ask. But after everything we'd been through, I figured I had a right to know. "Daren, what happened to Dean?"

"He went after a spider when we were working on the tree house. He lost his footing and fell." Daren paused to look at the cross in the tall grass. "I got down as fast as I could. I thought he'd be OK. He could talk . . . squeeze my hand." Daren stared at his deformed fingers, living it again. "Then he closed his eyes and . . ."

"I'm sorry, Daren." I said softly. I shifted my attention to the weeds on the ground below. "I can't believe your parents still let you come up here."

"It took a while," Daren shrugged. "But they know how much it means to me. Plus, we don't live that far away." He pointed to a well-kept two-story house, just visible through the trees.

"After Dean died, I quit building the tree house," Daren went on. "I just came back to kill spiders. I was good at it. I stomped on them. Poisoned them. Made them suffer. But the weird thing was, I didn't feel any better. I felt guilty, like I was just as cruel as everyone else."

"You're the one I saw in the library getting chased."

"Dean would always stick up for me . . ." Daren looked away, but couldn't hide the hurt. "I think the librarian feels sorry for me. She finds room in the budget for extra spider books. Lets me keep them past due."

"I don't get it," I told him. "You said you hated spiders."

"I did. Then one day I came here to get away from some kids. I fell asleep hiding. When I woke up, a spider was on my hand. It crawled all over it, back and forth, in no hurry to leave." Daren showed me his right hand. It only had two fingers, double the normal size. His palm rolled together. "Maybe the spider thought I was related. It kind of looks like a spider's leg, huh?"

I shrugged and tried not to stare. But I didn't do a very good job.

"Don't worry about it," Daren said when he noticed my discomfort, "I was born with my hand like this. I'm kind of used to it by now." He smiled at me and modeled his deformed hand, continuing his story. "The weird thing was, I didn't want the spider to leave. When it crawled off, I picked it up again. Then something clicked. I realized I had been treating spiders like everyone else treated me. That's when I changed. I started reading about spiders. I learned how they spin webs and what they eat. I learned how to catch them without hurting them by using a soft net. I figured out where they hide when they're not sitting in their webs."

"You took them away, didn't you?" I remembered when we can to the tree and all the spiders were gone. "You overheard us talking about using pesticides."

Daren confessed that it had taken him hours to catch all the spiders. "I couldn't let you kill them. I brought them here, I had to protect them. They're my pets."

"Your pets?" I cringed. "Spiders?"

"I know that seems weird. People hate spiders just because of the way they look. But that's not a good reason to hate anything . . . or anyone."

Daren drew my attention to his deformed hand. That's when I got it. Daren saw himself in the spiders, picked on because of the way he looked. That's why he protected the spiders at any cost; he was to them what Dean was to him.

"The spiders belong here," Daren went on. "You saw what happened when I took them away."

"The mosquitoes were terrible. So were the flies." I watched a red spider on a nearby branch. "So you went from killing to collecting, just like that?"

"Not just like that. It took time. I kept reading. Eventually, I made connections with other collectors."

"Like Mr. Scopula?"

"No, that was me. I'm sorry I lied to you about the Giant Orb Weaver."

I didn't know what to say. I felt anger and pity at the same time. Conner could have been killed. I searched for the perfect comeback. All that came out was, "I forgive you."

Daren grabbed an overhead branch with his deformed hand and did a pull up. I think he wanted me to see that his hand wasn't useless—just the opposite. His two fingers reminded me of a sloth's claw. But he didn't move like a sloth. When I asked him how he learned to climb so fast, he told me it took practice and time. Eventually, he had learned every foothold in the tree, and how to shinny straight up when there wasn't one. He figured out where to jump and where to hide. He used a climber's harness and white nylon rope to create the illusion of swinging from a web.

Daren disappeared in the widow's watch. I heard movement of some kind—glass, twigs, stuff shifting. "Do you want to come up here?"

"Um . . ." Before I could object, Daren dropped a rope ladder over the side.

I gave it a tug. It seemed sturdy enough, so I climbed up and into the widow's watch.

A faded piece of carpet rested on top of the floor branches. Daren sat cross-legged in the corner. A framed picture of Dean hung from the half wall. Glass jars held all kinds of spiders. Some green. Others bright yellow. A tarantula rested in Daren's lap. A spider mask and fuzzy brown clothes were piled next to him, along with a vinyl sleeve that came to a point at the end. The spider's leg.

I pointed to a plastic container next to Conner's box of nails. "Are more spiders in there?"

"That's road kill. It attracts flies." He explained what went into caring for the spiders. His pets. I felt guilty. He was right about what we would have done to them.

The idea that someone cared about them—or that God created spiders for a reason—would never have crossed my mind. I had one word for them. Gross.

Daren must have read my mind. He got out a granddaddy longlegs for me to hold.

"No way," I said.

"Don't worry. It's not deadly. None of them are." He let it walk up and down his arm.

"Gross." I slapped my hand over my mouth. "You didn't hear that."

"Yes, I did. You owe a quarter."

I grinned and watched the spider. "You're sure about this?"

"Positive." He let it walk to his hand, then put it on mine. I tensed up and repressed a squeal. I whispered my verse. The spider moved to my wrist. Carefully. More afraid of me than I was of it. I let out a breath and calmed down. Its legs were like angel hairs and seemed too thin to support its round body. It tickled as it walked back and forth. It was hard to believe that something so delicate had always scared me to death.

"I think it likes you," Daren told me. He returned the granddaddy longlegs to its jar.

That was my cue to take in the view. I could see our big yard and Victorian house. For some reason it looked better, and I had a pretty good idea why. I had always looked at it in the same way I had looked at spiders, and Daren's hand, and everything. Superficially. But at least I understood that about myself. And with God's help, I could change.

"So, have you made any friends yet?" Daren asked.

I shook my head. I told him about our move and how hard it had been.

"You can hang out with me if you want."

I thanked him and told him I would.

His eyes lit up. "Really?"

"Sure, let's shake on it." I extended my right hand.

He looked at his, with its deformed fingers and curled palm. Then he looked back at me. I just left my hand there. He extended his slowly. Uncertainly. I grabbed hold and gave it a squeeze, in no rush to let go. Daren smiled, like that was the nicest thing I could have done.

And best of all, the G word never even crossed my mind.

Don't Miss another exciting

HEEBIE JEEBIES

adventure!

Turn the page to check out a chapter from

DANCES WITH WEREWOLVES

Chapter 1

I looked out the car window. Pine trees whizzed by on the winding mountain road. They looked just like all the other pine trees we'd been driving through for the past hour. I tried the car radio, but all I got was static, so I switched it off. I rolled the window down a little and sniffed the clean mountain air everyone's always talking about.

"Everything up here smells like sawdust," I told my mom. "Is that how it's supposed to smell?"

Mom just laughed. I rolled the window up again.

I'm twelve, and twelve is old enough to take care of myself, but I've got to admit that the prospect of spending a month at a camp in the boonies makes me nervous. What if I don't make any friends? What if the other kids are mean to me? What if I get homesick? What if I get lost in the woods? I felt a lump growing in my throat.

My trip to Teepee Village Summer Camp is the first time I've really been away from home. Sure, I've been to a few sleepovers at friends' houses, and I've stayed at my grandmother's house a couple of weeks. But this is different. At Teepee Village, I'm going to be on my own.

Mom says I'm going to have the time of my life. She says I'll get over my homesickness before I know it. She insists I'll have more fun at summer camp than I would lying around the house watching television all day. She predicts I'll make lifelong friends. I don't know about that.

This is also the first time I've really been out in the boonies. I live in the city and the closest thing to camping I've ever done is a picnic in the park.

"There's nothing to worry about," Mom said, as if she could read my mind. "You'll have a great time. By tomorrow afternoon you'll know plenty of people. The boys in your teepee will seem like old friends before you know it."

I looked out the window again. The woods were thick and dark and mossy. "Are there any bears up here?" I asked Mom.

"Not in these hills," she said.

"Any mountain lions or rattlesnakes?"

Mom smiled. "Nope. It's perfectly safe. There are no dangerous animals in these parts." She glanced over at me, her eyes sparkling. I could tell she was thinking that I was still her little boy. I could tell she wanted to reach over and muss my hair. "This will be good for you," she assured me. "You'll finally get acquainted with nature."

"I know plenty about nature," I told her. "We get it on cable."

Mom laughed. "Yeah, you're a real woodsman, you are."

"Any hyenas up here?" I asked. "Man eating sharks?"

Mom laughed again. "Like I said: There are no dangerous animals in these woods."

Boy, was she ever wrong.